Injury

VAL TOBIN

To Carmela,
Hope you enjoy
the story!
Val Tobin

DEDICATION

To Bob, Jenn, Mark, Chanelle, Savannah, Jack, and, of course, Robert "Cope" Copeland

ACKNOWLEDGMENTS

Editing by Kelly Hartigan (XterraWeb) editing.xterraweb.com. Thank you, Kelly.

Thanks to Patti Roberts of Paradox (paradoxbooktrailerproductions.blogspot.com.au/) for the amazing cover.

Thanks also to Andrea Holmes, Val Cseh, Michelle Legere, Kathy Rinaldo, Heather Tobin, Kelly-Marie Murtha, Angel Morgan, John Erwin, Judy Flinn, Alis Kennedy, Bob Holmes, the OPP officer, and Sergeant Kelly Bachoo, York Regional Police.

CHAPTER 1

Eyes closed, a sheet covering her face, Daniella Grayson groped for the phone and dragged the receiver to her ear. "Hello?"

"This is Tobey Ames from TNN, Miss Grayson. Do you have any comment on last night's arrest of your mother?"

Were she not so hung over, Dani would've bolted up. Instead, she drew her legs to her chest, assuming the fetal position.

"No comment." The hand that held the phone dropped to the bed. Thumb probing for the "End" button, she found it and disconnected the call.

The phone rang again as she contemplated whom to call first. This time, she let it go to voice-mail. The machine in the living room clicked on after the third ring. The message and beep played, and John Madden, her manager, came on, sounding intense.

"Dani. Are you screening? Pick up. I've been fielding calls about your mother ..."

She sat this time, resting her aching head on bent knees, and answered. "What's going on? Tobey Ames just called, asking about my mother's arrest."

"I don't know the details yet. They're accusing your mother of killing your father twenty years ago. You would have been what, then? Five?"

Silence. Dani tried to understand what she'd heard.

"My father left us when I was five." Her mouth went dry, and her hands and feet grew cold. "Lilli was a bitch from hell." Nausea threatened and her spine prickled as she processed the awful news. *Could it be possible? Oh, God.* "She's capable of it. If they've arrested her for killing Daddy, she probably did it." An edge of hysteria had crept into her voice.

"Listen," John said. "Don't answer the phone or open the door until I get there. I'll call the lawyer on my way over, and we'll figure this thing out.

1

There must be a mistake."

Dani said goodbye and hung up the phone. She shivered as she slipped out from under the covers and got out of bed. A glance at the clock on her nightstand showed seven-twenty in the morning. No wonder she felt like shit—she'd just gotten *into* bed at four-thirty, helped up to her apartment once again by her trusty chauffeur. *What's his name?* She always had trouble remembering. *Oh, yeah, Cope.*

Good looking as hell, but too young for Dani's tastes, and her employee, so she barely gave him a second glance. But he was kind and helpful and made sure she got home safely no matter how drunk she was.

She grabbed her bathrobe and snuggled her naked body into the warm terry cloth. As she slid her feet into a pair of slippers, the phone rang again. She returned to her nightstand and disconnected the phone. It continued to ring in the living room until the machine kicked in.

She listened for the caller's voice.

"Hello, Miss Grayson. It's Mark Rutherford of ASN. John Madden suggested you give me an exclusive interview. I'd love to hear your side of the story. Please call me back at ..."

Dani shook her head in disgust while Rutherford recited his phone number. She pulled the plug on the living room phone as well. Anyone she'd want to talk to could call her cell.

She sank onto the couch, switched on the TV, and clicked over to the news channel. An eternity seemed to pass before the stories cycled to the one about her mother. Finally, the newscaster returned to the headline news.

A somber Toby Ames faced the camera, eyes filled with compassion. "Ms. Lillian Capshaw, mother of Oscar-winning actress Daniella Grayson, was arrested last night in her apartment in Toronto on charges of first degree murder in the death of her husband Paul Grayson. Grayson's skeletal remains were discovered yesterday morning in a capped well at a Sharon, Ontario, residence once rented by the family. Ms. Capshaw was taken into custody late last night."

Dani's childhood home flashed on the screen behind the reporter. Plywood covered the windows, and two police cars sat in the driveway. Video footage of Dani appeared on the screen next, showing her exiting a limousine.

The newscaster continued in voiceover. "Miss Grayson, seen here arriving at the premiere of her movie, the Academy Award-winning best picture *Injury*, lives in Los Angeles and has not commented on last night's events. We will update you as the story progresses."

Dani flicked to a channel that focused more on entertainment news. After a few minutes, her photo appeared behind the news anchor, and he gave the same spiel as Ames had though without the premiere clip.

The footage then switched to a taped interview with Gregory Henderson, caught leaving a restaurant with a date. Dani swallowed past a lump in her throat and hugged herself, terrified of what her former boyfriend and costar might say.

Always an attention hog, Henderson leaned toward the female reporter and into the microphone. "No, I haven't talked to Dani. She's not speaking to me these days."

Dani noted the slight slur in his speech. Henderson's arm rested around the shoulders of a gorgeous blonde, who looked delighted to be with him, getting her fifteen minutes of fame.

"Did you meet Lilli Capshaw when you were dating Miss Grayson?"

"No ma'am." Henderson swayed and steadied himself by leaning on his date. "Dani kept me all to herself." He looked into the camera. "Call me, sweetheart. I'm here for you, baby."

The date lost her look of delight.

After a few more inane questions from the reporter and more slurred responses from Henderson, the interview wrapped up.

What an ass. Dani switched off the television, recalling the premiere. She'd stepped out of the limousine and had smiled for the cameras while voices of people she didn't know had cried out for her to look their way.

She hooked her arm through Henderson's and hoped her four-inch heels wouldn't catch on the red carpet.

"Greg," she whispered, "don't let go of my arm."

He smiled at her. "Relax, baby. I've got you covered."

Dani loved tall men. At five-foot-ten, she usually looked most men in the eyes—looked down on them, let's be honest—especially in four-inch heels. Henderson was the perfect height for her, and their chemistry on screen and high-profile romance off screen had helped make *Injury* the hit of the season.

She tried to get in front of the cameras as much as possible and had worked hard at looking particularly stunning for that premiere. Her body-hugging gown had shown off her slender figure. She'd let her long, dark hair hang loose in a wild and carefree way that took hours with a curling iron to achieve.

Maybe my father is watching this, she'd thought, as she always did when she put herself on display in public. It's *why* she put herself on display in public.

Daddy's never seen me. All those times, I thought he'd see me and feel sorry he left us, and he wasn't even alive.

The doorbell rang. *John.*

She unfurled from the couch and waited for him to enter. When the door didn't open, she walked over, reached for the deadbolt, and then remembered John's warning to not open the door. She checked the peephole. Nothing there. If that was John, he wouldn't be hiding. She waited. The doorbell rang again, but whoever was there took pains not to be seen.

Dani left the door, went to her room, and opened her closet. *There'll be a media feeding frenzy. What am I going to wear?*

Did it matter? Yes, she supposed it did, but it felt strange to know that her father wasn't out there somewhere, perhaps noticing her and thinking about contacting her.

At eighteen, she'd tried to find him, to ask him why he'd turned his back on her. She could understand that he'd want to escape controlling, abusive, obsessive Lilli. Dani herself had moved out of her mother's home at sixteen. But Dani was a child when her dad had disappeared, and she'd taken the rejection and ensuing lack of contact personally.

The knocking on the door penetrated her thoughts. *How'd that asshole get into the building?* Multiple fists pounded the door, she realized. More than one asshole was out there in the hall stalking her. Then she heard voices arguing, demanding. She hopped back into bed, pulled the covers under her chin, and waited.

A key rattling in the door told her John had arrived. Dani sighed and slid out of bed. Peering out of her bedroom, she waited for him to step inside. John: handsome, rugged, older. But assertive, protective, kind. She itched to touch him.

Would he sleep with her now she was over twenty-one? It'd been five years since she'd tested those waters. When she'd first hired him to be her manager, she'd thrown herself at him.

She'd almost fired him when he'd rejected her, then had decided she didn't give a shit after all. One by one, she'd seduced his associates, until she'd gotten it out of her system. The older men had been eager to accept the offer of her young body.

When John had complained, like he had any right to say anything about whom she fucked, she'd told him to butt out. He'd almost quit on her then, and she'd had to beg and plead and promise the moon to keep him as her manager. Fear of him abandoning her reined in her reckless, wanton behavior, and she'd battled to keep him in her life.

They'd had a holy alliance since then, focusing on her career, which had skyrocketed. She'd kept her attraction to him locked away, taking it out only in the darkest of nights when she took comfort from and pleasured herself on thoughts of him.

But now that ache for him was back, fierce, hot. Dani slid a hand down her robe and loosened the knot on the belt at her waist. The robe parted slightly, exposing her body in a thin, vertical line of curves and shadows. Her nipples hardened, and she parted her lips.

She tilted her head to the side and watched John struggle to shut the door as hands holding microphones jammed themselves into the opening, and voices shouted her name. John pushed against the door, and a man cried out in pain. The arms disappeared, and the door slammed shut.

"Don't worry. I've alerted security. They'll be gone soon," John said, his back to her.

The normality of seeing him there shook her back to reality, and she closed the robe. When he turned to her, she faced him head on.

"John." Her voice caught in her throat, and his name came out low and throaty, but it was grief, not lust, that did it. "What happened to my father?"

CHAPTER 2

John moved closer to Dani, and her heart leapt at the thought he might touch her.

His arms hung at his sides and stayed there. Heat from his body made her insides tingle.

She stepped nearer and breathed in his scent. "Is it true?"

He stood kissing-close to her now. She gazed into his deep, brown eyes and smelled mint on his breath. Stubble roughened his chin and cheeks. He hadn't shaved. He must have jumped out of bed and raced over to her without doing much more than getting dressed and brushing his teeth.

John placed a hand on each side of her face, sending electrical pulses down her body.

Blood roared in her ears, and her heart pounded.

His expression showed confusion, but his eyes betrayed his pain and sorrow.

"It's true. They found his remains on the property your family rented. They gathered enough evidence to charge Lilli with murder. Paul Grayson's been dead twenty years."

Dani's head throbbed, pounding in time to her heartbeat. It couldn't be true.

"No." Not knowing how else to take solace, she put her arms around John.

He pressed her head to his chest and stroked her hair. "I understand you're overwhelmed. I'll help you get through this. I love you, and I care about you."

He'd always been there for her, guiding her career, seeing her through the tough times and the good times. He'd picked up the pieces when her relationships with the men she carried on with fell apart, and he understood her better than anyone.

The times she was at her lowest, John had been there to support and encourage her. Even her own mother had told her she was useless and too fat and ugly to make it. John had dragged Dani back from the brink of anorexia, from the thoughts of suicide, from the pills and the coke—able to help her because he was her trusted friend. She stopped crying and hugged him tight.

One of his arms folded around her shoulders and his hand cupped the back of her head. "We'll get through this, honey."

"Okay. I'll be fine. Thanks." She looked up at him. "What did the lawyer say?"

"Nothing good. She did it." He led her to the couch in the living room, and they sat.

"Lilli's going away, isn't she?"

"Yes. The trial will decide that, of course, but the lawyer said she's claiming self-defense."

Dani leaned against John, and he drew her in close, making her feel safe.

"Daddy didn't leave me." She said it out loud, practicing it, trying it on. Head pounding, she closed her eyes and slept.

***

When Dani opened her eyes again, she was lying on the couch, a blanket draped over her. Her head no longer throbbed. Golden light spilled in through the windows, making her squint. She sat up and searched for John. When she didn't see him, she called out.

The door of her office opened, and he stepped out, cell phone pressed to his ear. "Yeah, thanks. She's up now. We'll get back to you."

She waited, brows arched, while he slipped his phone back into the case on his hip.

"Hungry?"

She didn't reply, expecting him to understand she wanted to know what was going on.

Distracted, he headed toward the kitchen, scratching his head.

"John," she called. "Don't you have something to tell me?"

He paused. "Yeah. But you should eat first."

"Fuck that. What is it?" Her voice filled with anxiety.

"Sorry. I don't want you to get upset." He frowned. "That was Jeanette."

Her agent. Probably a proposal, but something must be wrong, or John wouldn't be so reluctant to discuss it.

His eyes narrowed. "The rep from Danger Play called."

Dani's heart skipped a beat at the mention of the studio that had funded *Injury* and held her contract. She knew what he'd say next and sucked in a breath.

"They're doing a sequel and want you back. Henderson, too. They're offering you nine million and revenue share." John strode to the couch and sat next to her. "The public's been clamoring for it. The studio got the green light and wants to begin filming next month if you agree to the terms. I can tell them you won't do it if Henderson comes back."

Dani stared at her hands, which rested in her lap. "The picture would suffer. If I do this, Greg will have to be there. They'll insist on it." She kept her head down, avoiding his eyes. John still didn't know the truth behind the breakup with Henderson, and she didn't want to talk about it now.

"You don't have to tell me what happened. But if you want me to agree to let you work with him again, you'll have to give me something. You act like you despise him. How do you think you'll convince anyone that your character loves him?"

"I'm the actress—let me worry about that. If it's not working, we'll find out soon enough."

"Think it through. Call me tomorrow morning with your decision. If you're up to it, Jeanette will get you the contract to sign."

"Okay." Probably better not to give them an answer now—she had more pressing things on her mind. Mouth dry, Dani licked her lips. She wanted a drink. The small bar next to the loveseat beckoned, and she went to it, gaze focused on the bottles standing at attention behind the glass door.

"What are you doing?" John's tone was brusque.

She paused. She'd been about to make a martini, and she hadn't had— what time was it, anyway? Dani checked the clock, which showed 6:03. She'd slept the day away? Again? "You've been here all day and let me sleep?"

"You needed it. No doubt, you were up all night. You haven't eaten anything, and you're reaching for a cocktail. I'm worried about your drinking. If I have to, I'll send you back to rehab."

Fury made her turn on him. "You don't get to tell me what to do. You're my manager, not my parent. I don't have any parents." Her voice sounded shrill. Tears threatened.

John covered the distance between them in two long strides.

She thought he'd hug her then, but he didn't.

Her body shook, and she wished he'd put his arms around her. She hungered for a touch—any touch. A flashback to five years ago when she'd tried to seduce him and he'd rejected her seared through her head.

"I'm going in the shower. When I get out, you'd better be gone." She didn't need him—she didn't need anyone. She was Daniella fucking Grayson. If she needed company, she could find it.

He scowled, and when she tried to break past him, he grabbed her by the arm.

"No. I'm not going anywhere until I know you won't tie one on when I leave. I understand you're going through a difficult time. That's why I'm here. Yell at me all you want. I'm not letting you ruin yourself no matter what that harpy of a mother did twenty years ago. Is that clear?"

Dani nodded, but he wasn't satisfied.

"Say it."

"I won't get drunk." But oh, Christ, she wanted a drink. This time, when John suggested making Dani something to eat, she agreed.

CHAPTER 3

A veggie omelet, a piece of toast, juice, and hot coffee filled her belly, and Dani fought the urge to run into the bathroom and throw it up. To keep her thoughts off the toilet, she collected their dishes and focused on cleaning up the meal.

The fear of getting fat and losing her career was a constant throb in her stomach and made eating difficult. Rehab and a therapist had helped to get it under control, but Dani found that when the stress backed up on her, the anxiety became almost impossible to manage.

"Thanks for breakfast. Dinner. Whatever." Head tilted toward her shoulder, she smiled at John, who sat on the couch in the living room.

"Glad to see you eating." He frowned, probably worrying she'd relapse. "Will you be okay?"

She eyed the bathroom door, an involuntary motion, and as soon as she realized what she'd done, she snapped her attention back to John. Would she ever be able to eat without that rising unease? "I don't starve myself anymore, and I don't throw up. I watch what I eat and I exercise. 'Kay?"

He joined her in the kitchen. "I'm worried about how you're coping. When's your next therapy appointment? If it's not tomorrow, make one with Doctor Hadley. Talk it through."

"I'm fine." Dani continued to rinse the dishes and stack them in the dishwasher.

"I saw the interview with Henderson. He told you to call him. If you agree to do the picture, you'll be working with him—and there'll be love scenes. Between that and everything that's happened this morning, you'll need a professional to talk to. Call Hadley. It's not showing weakness to see a therapist—it's a way to stay strong."

She didn't reply, just dumped soap into the dishwasher, snapped it closed, and turned it on. It ran silently, the humming fridge the loudest sound in the room. A glance at John showed him waiting for her response.

"Last night, I had a few drinks with friends. I'm not an alcoholic."

"Said every alcoholic in the history of alcoholics."

She shot dagger eyes at him. "The drinking is under control. I stopped, no problem, before, and I can do it again. You know I don't drink when I'm working on a picture. Even Hadley said I'm not an alcoholic. I don't have all the signs, but I do have to be aware of what I'm doing to deal with my problems."

"As soon as you woke up this evening, you wanted a drink. You've already had one DUI. When do you get your license back?" Hands fisted on his waist, John leaned toward her, face flushed.

She sighed. "Three months. All right, I get it. When the news about my mother broke, it shook me up. Most people dealing with that would want a drink. Give me a break, okay? And I'm paying for what I did when I was dating Greg Henderson."

"What are your plans for tonight?"

"Liz is coming over. Don't worry. If we go out, we'll behave."

John frowned again. "Will you tell her about the sequel?"

"Yes. She'll want to audition, and I'll help her get a part."

Elizabeth Logan and Dani had met five years before on an audition that, for Dani, had been a disaster. Sick with the flu, she'd shown up to the audition anyway because rent was due and she had no money.

The waiting did her in.

Crowded into a holding area with fifty other hopefuls, Dani forced herself to sit straight. She tried to look like the character she wanted to play: a confident, powerful young leader of a youth group who would one day become president. Liz, seated next to Dani, chatted with her to help take her mind off the nausea.

All their efforts shot to hell when the casting director called Dani into the room. She threw up on the floor in front of him, the meager contents of her stomach splashing onto his shoes. She left the room in tears and huddled in the bathroom for the next two hours.

After her audition, Elizabeth coaxed Dani away from the toilet, helped her get home, and then lent her rent money.

They'd run into each other at subsequent auditions and struck up a close friendship even though they competed for the same parts. When Dani's career took off after the success of *Injury*, Liz admitted a touch of envy, but Dani vowed her friend would benefit from the good fortune.

Dani unabashedly used her star power to help Liz get ahead. Since then, she'd landed great roles and carried them well. In the meantime, the two young women enjoyed the attendant party life.

John picked up his jacket and put it on. "You going to call her, then?" To make sure, he waited.

She didn't know whether to be grateful or resentful. *Grateful.* He cared about her even if he wasn't in love with her. She picked up the phone and called Liz, who said she was on her way.

That settled, John said his goodbyes, and Dani walked him to the door. "What if they're still out there?"

"The reporters? They won't be in the hallway. I had security take care of that. But no doubt they'll be hanging around outside the building." He paused. "Warn Liz. She'll get swarmed."

Dani hugged him, brushing her lips against his cheek for a chaste kiss. When he'd left, she wandered back to the TV. Should she turn it on? She wasn't sure what had happened with her mother. No one had called her. Yet. She fully expected the police investigating the murder to contact her.

While she contemplated, the phone rang. John must have plugged it back in. Voice-mail picked up, and she listened to herself telling the caller she wasn't available. After the beep, a woman spoke. *Jeanette.* Dani snatched up the receiver. "I'm here. Just screening."

Jeannette's sexy voice, deep and throaty from years of smoking, floated through the receiver. "So glad to hear your voice. Are you okay? Sorry about your mother. What a shock."

"I'm fine." Dani folded herself onto the couch, legs curled under her.

"Did John mention the sequel?"

"Yes. I'm considering it."

"What's to consider? Darling, nine million dollars. And a share in the revenues. This is a sure thing."

"Henderson and I have issues. John suggested I think it over—maybe demand to have him written out of the picture."

"You'll be fine. You're both professionals. Why didn't you tell me you two were having problems? Was it that bad?" Jeannette's voice held fear.

Dani couldn't tell if it was fear of her backing out of the series or fear for her if Greg came back into her life. "He was toxic. That's all I'll say."

"The studio wants both of you. They won't be okay with writing him out of it. You'll risk everything. You know these guys: they can make or break you. Piss them off, and your career, which is in the stratosphere, will tank. They'll offer you shitty, dumb-blonde parts."

"I'm not blonde." Dani smiled.

"That's not funny. They'd make you dye it and give you vacuous parts that damage your career."

"There are other studios."

"You're still under contract with this one for at least four more films. Don't fuck with them." Jeanette sounded desperate now, and a shiver of dread bolted through Dani.

"He has bizarre tastes. I can't get involved with him again." She didn't want to talk about him anymore. It brought back too many unsavory memories. What would seeing him every day for months do to her?

"Are you saying you're pulling out? Because that won't fly. What would make it easier for you to say yes?"

Dani considered how to respond. Silence hung heavy. Jeannette's breath puffed into Dani's ear, and she realized the agent was smoking. "Do they know there's a problem?" *Of course, the studio knows.* The execs had watched the relationship implode during the promotional tour for *Injury.*

George Manning, Danger Play head, had hauled both Dani and Greg into his office during a break in their marketing travels. He ordered them to get over it, or he'd sue them both. Dani had done as directed, avoiding Henderson whenever possible, and linking arms and canoodling with him in public when the job demanded.

But she'd been more naïve then, lacking confidence, and did whatever the older and, she assumed, wiser adults around her told her to do. It had never occurred to her to consult with a lawyer.

Why hadn't John stepped in and defended her? But she brushed that aside as soon as she thought it. John hadn't accompanied her on that tour, and she hadn't confided in him. He still didn't know the truth, and Dani liked it that way.

When the silence dragged on too long, she broke it. "What did they say?"

"They insist on the two of you. John should have told you how critical it is to accept this role as offered, including Henderson's presence. You're both adults. Rise above your personal issues and do your job. The pool of big-name celebrities right for that role is small. They can't replace Henderson with another actor—Greg owns that role. And they sure as hell don't want to write him out."

Jeanette took a long drag on her cigarette and continued. "I'm not saying you can't carry the film, but the magic happened because of the chemistry between you and Greg. I don't suppose you could date him just for the duration of the filming and the tour? How bizarre could his tastes be? A little BDSM? It's all the rage now. Most women would kill to be with him."

"No, I can't. He's an asshole, and I don't want to date him, not even for nine million dollars. I can't believe you're asking me to do this." Yet when John had suggested she back out of it, she'd argued. Why was she now fighting against doing it?

John was right. Dealing with that narcissist daily would be stressful. She recalled Henderson's expression when he stared into the camera and spoke directly to Dani during the interview she'd seen on TV earlier, and her stomach clenched.

Call me, sweetheart. I'm here for you, baby.

The public thought he was a romantic figure she'd jilted. *Damn him.* Call him? *No, Greg, I don't fucking think so. Sweetheart.*

"Darling? Are you there?" Jeanette's voice cut through Dani's musings.

"I'm here."

"Want to tell me what happened?" She sounded serious now. Dani detected a note of compassion, and it calmed her.

"No. I'll say he was a jerk and leave it at that. He's not dangerous." *He's not dangerous.* That was something she'd told herself daily after they'd gone their separate ways. She wanted to believe it, because if it wasn't true, she was a coward for not reporting him, and another woman might suffer for it.

"He's not dangerous," she repeated, convincing herself. "But he's bad for me. He's controlling, jealous."

"Oh, well, he was smitten with you. The whole world could tell he had goo-goo eyes for you. Did he hurt you?"

"Not so I should press charges." She paused again. She'd just given Jeanette a big broad hint at the truth and hoped the agent would miss it. To Dani's relief, Jeanette did—or she chose to overlook it.

"Well, that's fine, then. If you two can play nice while the picture shoots and during the marketing tour, then we'll all get a nice chunk of money from it. Shall I tell the studio to send the contract over? You can sign it tomorrow. They want to start production next month."

"Can I give you an answer in the morning?"

Dani heard a loud sigh, and it wasn't Jeanette taking another puff of her smoke.

"This should just be a formality. The studio is under pressure to get this film off the ground. If you drag your heels on it, they'll be upset with you. Four movies, remember? Who pays your bills? Who made you a star? Do you want to be labeled difficult?"

The threat behind Jeannette's words wasn't an empty one, and Dani knew it. She could handle Henderson—she wasn't a naïve girl anymore. She couldn't afford to make a misstep in her career, and she had to keep the studio happy. When she'd fulfilled her obligations, and her contract came up for renewal, she could consider going elsewhere.

"Okay, Jeanette. Tell them I'm in. Has Greg's agent replied?" Maybe Henderson would turn it down, though Dani suspected he'd jump at it.

"I haven't heard. But that's great news. I'll call the studio right away. Talk later."

Dani hung up the phone and eyed the liquor cabinet. She wasn't working on a film; she could have one drink. It's not like she'd get snockered. Besides, Liz was on her way over, and they'd go out to a club. Of course, they'd have a drink while they hung out. Dani fixed her gaze on the liquor bottles and decided to have the martini John had denied her earlier.

CHAPTER 4

Robert "Cope" Copeland sat at the bar watching Dani and Liz gyrate around the dance floor. He'd worked for four years for the limo company Dani's manager used to procure drivers. He'd been driving Dani around and doubling as her bodyguard since she'd lost her license three months ago. Before that, he'd been an occasional driver for her during the filming and promotion of *Injury*. Not that she'd remember. She'd been plowed most of that time.

At first, he'd thought the job akin to babysitting a spoiled rich brat, and he should know—he used to be one. But she'd turned out to be different than the average nobody thrust into wealth and fame at a young age. Dani didn't act spoiled, and she didn't throw money around. She was beautiful, of course, and he'd felt the pull of her charisma luring him in. He'd lusted after her from day one, but he'd kept it in check. The income from the job was more important than any woman right now.

Cope wanted to own his own limo company and worked long hours to save up the money he'd need to get it off the ground. A graduate of UC Berkeley with an MBA, Cope wanted to build the business himself, though his parents were wealthy enough to help him out. His mother pestered him to let them give him the money every time he visited.

But he knew there'd be a steep price to pay if he conceded—and not in cash. They'd own him, probably swallow his company whole, merging it with the rest of their conglomerate. That had happened to his older brothers, and Cope had concluded it wasn't for him.

A coffee in front of him, Cope let his gaze follow the girls as they wove around the other dancers. Almost all eyes were on them, and they made a gorgeous pair. Both young women wore short dresses that hugged their bodies. Their spike heels threw them off balance, giving a sexy sashay to their hips.

They never glanced at him, which was typical. To Cope's chagrin, Dani remained oblivious to his existence if she wasn't telling him where she wanted to go. He suspected she didn't even remember his real name half the time though he'd helped her up to her apartment often enough after a night of hard partying.

At least this night looked tame compared to the usual antics the girls got up to. But since he'd had to rein in an attraction to her, had behaved himself, the least she could do was acknowledge he existed. He knew he wasn't her type, which was anyone old enough to be her father. Cope figured he'd never be in the running whether he worked for her or not. He was only four or five years older than she was.

A guy standing on the sidelines, swaying drunk, leered at Dani.

Cope scowled.

In here, a place frequented by celebrities, no one pestered her for an autograph. The management frowned on it, and anyone harassing the patrons would get ejected. Outside she was fair game, and Cope had helped her dodge the reporters and fans vying for her attention when they'd first arrived. There had been far more of them than usual since the news of her mother's arrest had broken. He'd assumed it would be a tame night once they got inside.

This guy looked like trouble though, and Cope would need to keep a close eye on him. Guys like that might try anything, including slipping her a roofie. The creep sidled closer to Dani and Liz.

Tan, wearing a tight-fitting black T-shirt and cargo pants, the letch crept nearer. One hand swept down to block his crotch from her view the closer he got to her. The jerk was trying to conceal the hard-on he sported.

Casually, Cope took a sip of his coffee without taking his eyes off Creepy Guy. Cope would wait and see Dani's reaction to the douche before interfering. Whatever his opinion of the guys Dani dated, it wasn't his right to interfere if she wanted the attention. After all, she'd dated that sleazebag Greg Henderson for months, and Cope could only stand back and watch. It had been like Bambi versus King Kong, and Cope had wanted to slug that giant ape on more than one occasion. Instead, he'd had to drive them around and call the son-of-a-bitch "Mr."

Creepy Guy had arrived at his target and tapped Dani on the shoulder. His lips moved, then Dani's as she replied to him, but she shook her head while she spoke, so that was good. The guy took her hand then, and Cope sat up straight, itching to jump over there.

She pulled away, again saying something and shaking her head. When the guy put his arm around her, Cope was off his barstool and at her side before Dani or Creepy Guy could make any other move.

"This guy bothering you, Miss Grayson?" Cope had to shout to be heard. His voice must have reached Dani loud and clear, because she threw him a relieved glance and nodded.

"You need to back off," Cope shouted, and he glared daggers at the arm around Dani.

Creepy Guy scowled and looked at Dani, who stepped away and moved closer to Cope. He put one arm around Dani and the other around Liz and drew them away from the dance floor, Creepy Guy glaring after them.

"You okay?" Cope looked from Dani to Liz.

They both nodded and smiled at him.

"Ready to leave?" He guided them toward the exit as he talked.

Dani checked the time and glanced at Liz. "Just after midnight. I don't mind packing it in."

Liz agreed, and Dani looked at Cope again. "Thanks for your help. Liz is coming to my place, so we can go straight there."

The women wanted to hit the bathroom first, so he waited for them, spending the time scanning the club for Creepy Guy. He huddled with two of his buddies on the other side of the dance floor. They threw Cope a glance or two and returned to their huddle.

Might be trouble. He regretted he wasn't licensed for concealed carry though he had a black belt in Judo. Impatient, he checked the hallway leading to the restrooms. It puzzled him how much time women could spend in there. The longer they hung out here, the greater the odds Creepy Guy would conclude Cope had robbed him of a sure thing. Not true, of course—Dani had rejected the guy, but he'd refused to recognize the signals.

Relieved to see Dani and Liz approaching, Cope waited for them to catch up to him. When they reached him, he linked arms with them and stepped outside. He insisted Dani and Liz wait by the entrance, near club security, while he went for the car.

He went around to the back of the building into the parking lot and found his path blocked by Creepy Guy and his two odious hangers on. One guy had a scar across his cheek, and all three were broader than Cope though not taller. The last guy looked pasty and more nervous than Creepy Guy and Scarface.

Cope scanned the area. No one in sight. Hard to believe the creep wanted to mix it up, but he probably saw the limo driver as an easy target since they outnumbered him. They didn't outmatch him though, and they weren't sober. For Cope, it would be like kicking rabid hamsters.

He shook his head. "You don't want to fight me."

"You think you're tough? There're three of us."

"I'm not interested in a fight. Go home. I'm on duty."

Creepy Guy sneered, and the three brutes braced as if to spring. Scarface was the biggest one, so Cope lunged at him first. No sense in waiting to let them decide when it would start. He smashed the heel of his hand into

Scarface's nose, and the guy dropped like a stone. Cope dodged, avoiding Creepy Guy and his pasty friend, then twisted, kicked, and sent the two men to the pavement.

All three looked stunned. Cope loomed over them. "Go home or I'll call the cops and have your sorry asses up on assault charges."

Creepy Guy was a tenacious little fuck—he actually argued about it. "We're the ones on the ground. You jumped first."

"Look up. The security cameras will show everything, including you guys greeting me in such a friendly way."

"What happened here?" *Daniella.*

Annoyed that the women hadn't waited by security as he'd instructed, Cope turned to Dani and waved her and Liz toward the limo. "Get in the car, ladies. These gentlemen came to see us off."

Cope, who hadn't even broken a sweat, watched while the three thugs struggled to their feet and dusted off.

Dani and Liz picked their way across the cement to the limo, and Cope opened the passenger door for them. The women climbed into the car, and he slammed shut the door. He spared the defeated men cursory glances while he jumped into the vehicle and pulled out of the parking spot.

The limo arrived in front of Dani's apartment before one, and Cope, leaving his four-ways flashing, let the women out in front of the building. No one was around, but he walked them through the lobby to the elevator anyway. While they waited for the doors to open, Dani turned to him.

"I'm sorry for the trouble you had. Thank you for coming to our rescue."

"No problem, Miss Grayson. In future, I'd appreciate it if you'd remain by security. It could have been worse."

"Yes. They could have hurt you. When you didn't return right away, we went to check on you." Her chin rose, and her eyes narrowed.

"I handled it. Next time you want to check on me, send security. I don't want you taking risks. Fans or reporters might have swarmed you." He sounded brusque even to his own ears, but the thought of the chance she'd taken angered him.

Dani frowned and averted her eyes. "Okay. I'm sorry. Thank you for helping us." She looked up and smiled at him, something that always lit up his insides. Gorgeous though the rest of her was, that smile was her crowning glory. He was helpless before it, and all he wanted to do when she turned it on him was kiss her.

To his relief, Liz spoke then, breaking the spell. "Yes, thank you. Who knows what would've happened if you weren't there? One jerky guy is annoying, but three of them is scary."

"It's my job, ma'am." As soon as the words left his lips, he wanted to kick himself. *Ma'am? It's my job, paired up with ma'am? Am I a middle-aged cop on an old detective show? Jesus.*

He wanted to bang his head against the wall. He could take down three guys without getting winded, but Daniella Grayson made him lose his shit.

When the women were safely behind the closed doors of the elevator, he watched the numbers tick off until the count stopped at the penthouse. Done for the night, Cope headed outside to the limo to return it to the station and clock out.

CHAPTER 5

Dani opened her eyes, glanced at the clock, and was relieved to see it was still early. No headache. She hadn't overindulged the night before. Liz was still asleep in the guest room—she'd had more to drink than Dani, who'd only had two drinks the whole night.

See, John? No problem.

But she wouldn't tell him she'd had even that much—why go there? She had it under control. It felt good to wake without a hangover. Next week, she'd be expected to participate in meetings and attend photo shoots and fittings. Best to get the hard partying out of her system by then.

The prospect of starting a new project excited her even if it meant working with Greg Henderson. She looked forward to sliding into the skin of a character, and Felicity Sanderson in *Injury* was one of her favorites.

Dani rose, showered, dressed, and went into the room she used as an office. She synced her phone with the calendar on her computer and called Luanne, her assistant.

Luanne had worked for Dani for the past two years. At first, it had been weird to have an older woman working for her. After a few weeks of letting her organize everything, Dani didn't know how she'd managed before.

When Luanne answered, Dani asked her to book a flight to Toronto for the next morning. She wanted to see her mother before shooting started. With that out of the way, she strolled to the kitchen to get coffee going.

The aroma of fresh ground Kona coffee wafting through the air brought Liz stumbling from the guest room. Mouth opened wide in a yawn, she perched on a barstool at the island in the kitchen and propped her chin on her hand.

"Protein shake?" Dani said.

"Sure. Chocolate, please." Liz glanced at the clock. "Oh, God. It's dawn. How are you up so early?"

"It's not dawn. It's already eight o'clock."

The blender sat on the counter by the fridge, and Dani plugged it in and prepared the shakes. She set Liz's in front of her and made a vegan berry shake for herself. The phone rang as Dani sat down at the kitchen table. The two women locked gazes.

"You going to get that?" Liz said when Dani made no move toward the phone.

"I'm screening." If the calls started up again, she'd have to disconnect the phones.

The voice-mail message ended, the beep sounded, and a male voice spoke: "Miss Grayson, this is Detective Aaron Vega of the Sharon County Police Department in Ontario. I'd like to speak with you about your mother. Please call me back—"

Dani skidded into the living room and snatched up the phone. "I'm here, Detective."

"Oh, Good morning. Sorry to bother you, Miss Grayson." He gave Dani a badge number, which penetrated the numbness flooding her, but floated from her mind by the time he stopped speaking.

"Do you have a few minutes?"

"Yes." She sank onto the couch, posture rigid. Behind her, the kitchen chair scraped on the floor and Liz's footsteps pattered toward the spare room.

"This call is being recorded. Sorry about your father. I'd like to talk to you about what you remember from that night."

"Not much. All these years I'd believed what Lilli had told me—that he'd left us." Not for the first time since she'd heard the news, Dani tried to recall everything from that night.

"I'd prefer if we spoke in person. Are you planning to visit Toronto anytime soon?"

"I'm flying out tomorrow."

"Great. I'd like to meet with you and get the details—whatever you remember."

When she agreed, he gave her his phone number, and she entered it into her cell phone. She told him she'd have her assistant get in touch to set up the meeting, ended the call, and hurried to the spare room.

Liz sat on the bed, chin resting on the top of her bent knees. "Are you okay?"

Dani nodded. "It was a cop asking about Lilli."

"Do you want to talk about it?"

"No. I want to go out."

Her friend climbed from the bed and walked to Dani's side, putting her arms around her. "Are you sure? If you want to just hang here, I'm okay with that."

"I'm not interested in hanging. Let's get the hell out of here. I don't want to dwell. There'll be plenty of time for that in Toronto."

"Okay. Lend me some clothes? I only have what I wore last night."

Dani grinned, grabbed Liz by the hand, and led her to the walk-in closet in the master bedroom.

"Help yourself."

Liz squealed and scurried into the closet, the size of a small bedroom, and trailed her hands over the racks of clothes.

They spent the next hour preparing to go out, Dani's stomach in a constant knot at the prospect of facing her mother soon.

CHAPTER 6

Dani stared through the glass divider at her mother. "Why did you kill Daddy and then blame me for his disappearance?"

Lilli averted her gaze, but kept the phone clutched to her ear. "I haven't seen you in a long time, baby. Thank you for sending money all that time."

"I don't want to discuss much with you, Lilli. Answer my question."

"Because of you. I couldn't handle you, and he was a lousy provider. You two, so cozy together. Was there funny business? I thought there was funny business."

Dani gaped, puzzled, until she realized what her mother implied. "Paul Grayson was the best dad any little girl could have. He never hurt or hit me. You did that. All you ever did was belittle him. I don't know why you married him. You acted like you hated him."

Lilli swept a lock of mousey-blonde hair away from the side of her face, then pressed the phone back to her ear. "We married when I got pregnant with you. Our parents were against it. I was sixteen. He was seventeen. We ran away from home and went from one shitty basement apartment to another."

"I only remember the house in Sharon. Answer my question. Why did you kill my dad and then tell me he left us?"

"What did you expect me to say? Do you think I'd tell a five-year-old kid I killed her father?"

"You didn't mind telling a five-year-old kid her father abandoned her."

At the sound of Dani's raised voice, the guard standing by the door glanced over.

She turned her back on him and continued to call out her mother. "You owe me an explanation."

"We argued about money. He couldn't support us, the useless bastard. He wanted to leave. He threatened me with a gun and said he'd take you

23

with him. I grabbed it, we fought, it went off, and the bullet got him." Lilli paused and stared at her hand resting on the table in front of her. She looked up at Dani again and resumed her story. "He wanted to kill me. It was him."

Dani kept her expression neutral, but inside, she seethed. She glared at her mother and said, "Why didn't you let him take me away? You never loved me, so why keep me there?"

Lilli gave her daughter a perplexed look, as though she didn't understand the question. "Well, because you were mine. He couldn't take what was mine."

"I need to leave." Dani stood, but before she hung up the phone, she said, "Don't expect any more money from me. I wish Daddy had taken me away with him. We'd all have been better off."

The guard looked up as Dani breezed past and walked out.

An hour later, in Sharon, a town north of Toronto, Dani had her driver park in front of the property where her family had lived when Dani was five. The house, a bungalow set on ten acres, sat neglected and boarded up, waiting to be demolished. She walked around back, past strands of police tape littering the lawn behind the house.

She strode across the backyard, glad she'd changed into flat-heeled boots before coming out here. The ground was soft and mucky and the air damp. Wind blew hair in her face, forcing her to constantly swipe at it. Attempts to tame it by tucking it behind her ears failed. She shivered, underdressed for the sharp chill air of an Ontario April day.

She approached the well, heart pounding. Dad's body had lain discarded at the bottom for twenty years. Tears threatened, and she swallowed to suppress them. The police still had her father's remains.

Remains. The word horrified her. Bones, she supposed. The flesh would have rotted off. Tears sprang to her eyes and spilled down her cheeks. In life, Lilli had treated Paul Grayson like garbage and had disposed of him with that same attitude. Now Dani would get whatever was left.

She'd arranged to have him cremated and shipped out to LA when the police were done. There'd be no funeral. Who would she invite? The man had disappeared for twenty years, and no one had cared enough to wonder why he never called.

A makeshift fence prevented her from getting near the well, and that was okay. Dani wasn't sure why she'd come here, except that it might provide closure. The police tape, the fence, and the signs of activity around the well made it real and final.

On the way back to the car, she noticed a board missing from one of the windows. Guilt made Dani glance around to verify no one was watching. The nearest house was so far down the road she couldn't see it. The surrounding fields, once rented out to farmers, now sat unused, overrun by dead weeds and grasses poking up green again after the long winter.

Dani crept to the window and looked inside what used to be her bedroom. Empty of furniture, wallpaper torn, carpeting so filthy it was impossible to tell the color, but in her head, she saw it the way it used to be. She'd had a small, white dresser across from the window. Her bed had stuck out into the middle of the room, halfway between the window and the far wall. She'd had a toy box with blocks and dolls next to a small bookcase holding a meager collection of children's books. An area rug had covered the hardwood floor beside her bed. The pale pink walls had been smudged and scuffed.

Her gaze wandering to the closet, Dani sucked in her breath. The door stood cracked open, and her heart raced at the sight of it. She jerked her face away from the window, her mind flashing back to her mother screaming at her, dragging her into ... Pain speared her head and the memory dissolved. A migraine coming on. She'd better get back to the car and go to the Sharon Police Station before it paralyzed her.

She turned from her childhood home and walked away.

***

Detective Aaron Vega greeted Dani outside his office, clasping the hand she offered him in both of his, while giving his coworkers the stink eye when they looked in her direction.

"Thank you for coming, Miss Grayson. Please, come with me."

She followed Vega down the hall and into a room obviously designed to soothe. A padded couch and two armchairs in neutral tones surrounded a wood coffee table. The room was painted in pale blue. Two end tables held potted plants. The scent of fresh-brewed coffee made Dani's mouth water.

"Please, have a seat."

"Thank you." She sat down on the couch, back straight, hands folded in her lap.

"May I fix you a coffee?" Vega strode to a table holding everything you'd need to make coffee or tea. "I'm having one myself." He set his briefcase on the floor, removed his jacket, and draped it over the back of a chair.

"Yes, please." She beamed a smile at him. "Black." Dani hoped it wasn't swill. Maybe it would help stave off the looming migraine.

She studied him while he poured coffee and exchanged pleasantries with her.

Tidy and composed, he wore a white shirt buttoned up to the neck, tie snugged tight against the collar. His shirt cuffs skimmed his wrists. No rolling up the sleeves for this guy. She guessed he was in his early forties, the tinge of gray in his military-short hair giving him a distinguished air. He had a sturdy, square jaw and classic nose though a small scar above his left eye gave him an air of danger.

A glance at his ring finger showed he was married. A shame. When she'd walked behind him, she'd noted the nicely formed butt and toned thighs that his dress pants didn't quite conceal. He had some fine lines, and his muscles pressed against his shirt when he moved.

He handed her a mug of coffee and sat in the armchair across from her.

"The room is equipped with video cameras, and they're recording." When she acknowledged the news with a nod, he stated the date, time, and participants. Preliminaries done, he looked up and met her gaze. "All right, Miss Grayson? Can I get you anything else?"

Dani sipped the coffee. It was okay. "I'm fine, thank you. Where would you like to start?"

"What do you remember from the last time you saw your father?" His voice was soft and calming, but firm.

"I remember my father putting me to bed, reading me a story. It was his job to get me to sleep. My mother didn't have patience for me." Her breath hitched at the memory of the last night she'd shared with her dad. Her daddy. She remembered a handsome, kind man, but maybe that was how every five-year-old thought of her father.

He'd been short in stature, but young Dani thought he was a giant. A beautiful, powerful giant, with dark hair, hazel-brown eyes, and a warm smile. Gentle by nature, soft spoken, he worked hard to keep the family sheltered, fed, and clothed. His seasonal work had him laid off every winter, something Lilli had resented.

"They fought," Dani said. "My dad was out of work. It was before Christmas, and he'd lost his job again. He worked in the construction industry, and when the outdoor jobs dried up, they let the workers go."

"What did you hear?"

She sighed. This part of the night was clear in her memory. "Shouting. Lilli did most of the yelling. Dad was a quiet guy. Didn't go out much—my mom saw to that. When he was working, we didn't see him, but when business got slow, he was around more, and she nagged him constantly."

"What did they fight about?"

"Work, mostly. She'd pick at him about other things, too, though. Nothing he did was right. Nothing was good enough."

"How did your father react to that?"

"He said he was trying his best. They didn't have programs in place for retraining then. He'd always find something to keep us going until spring, but it took time. I think this time they had more debts, and the holidays were approaching, so Lilli wanted money fast."

"What happened then?"

"It's hard for me to remember. I was in my bed. Daddy tucked me in, read me a story, gave me a kiss, and went to watch TV. Then I heard her shouting at him. After that, I don't know. My next recollection is of coming home from school the next day and Lilli telling me Daddy left us and wasn't coming back." Tears rolled down Dani's cheeks, and she held her breath, willing herself not to sob.

Vega offered her a box of tissues from the table, and she took one and pressed it to her eyes.

"It's okay. Lilli didn't tell you why he was gone or where he went?"

"She said—" Dani's voice broke then, and she sobbed out loud.

"I'm sorry, Miss Grayson. Take your time. It's important we find out what happened, and as far as I know, you're the last person other than your mother to see Paul Grayson alive."

A stifled sob choked her, so Dani inhaled, held her breath for a moment, and then let it out in a burst. "Okay. Thank you." She paused before continuing. "It's difficult to talk about what she said. My mother was rarely kind. That day, I went to kindergarten in the morning. Lilli took me. My father wasn't around, I recall now."

"Did you ask where he was?"

"No. Not then. I got ready for school, Lilli rushing me, and we left the house."

"Did she rush you more than usual?"

"Not that I noticed."

"Anything unusual about her that morning?"

"I don't think so."

"Okay. What happened when you came home?"

"She met me at school and brought me home. When we walked in the door, she turned to me and said, 'Your father's gone, and he's not coming back. It's your fault. He doesn't want to bother with raising a kid.' She said it just like that and then turned and walked away. When I cried, she screamed at me to shut up, put my lunch on the table, and went to her room." Dani fell silent.

"I'm so sorry, Miss Grayson."

She found his sympathy reassuring. "Please, call me Dani. I'm telling you things I've told no one before. You might as well use my first name."

"Okay, Dani. Anything else you can tell me about that night or the next day?"

"No. We carried on without my dad. If I cried in front of her, she screamed at me, so I learned to cry at night when I was alone. I missed my dad and thought about him every day after that, always hoping that someday he'd contact me." Tears threatened again and she stopped talking, a lump growing in her throat.

"It must be hard for you. Did anything happen in the days and weeks that followed to indicate something wasn't right with Lilli?"

She almost laughed aloud at that. "Nothing was right with Lilli, Detective. Nothing was ever right with Lilli. She was as mean as ever. I don't know why she didn't get rid of me, too." The lump in her throat wanted to strangle her, and her chest was a tight band of hurt. "I'm sorry. That's all I remember." Her voice was a whisper.

"Here's my card. If you think of anything else, please call me."

It appeared in front of her face, and she tugged it from his fingers and shoved it into her purse.

"I'm sorry you have to deal with this."

"Thank you." She expected him to tell her she could leave, but the silence dragged on while she sipped coffee. She looked up to find him staring at her, his face red.

"Dani." He stopped.

Fear lanced through her, and she felt the blood drain from her face. "What's wrong?"

"I'm sorry. Nothing." Vega set his mug on the table and stood. "I was wondering if I could get your autograph. My wife and kids would be thrilled."

Dani exhaled, relieved. "Of course. I'm sorry, but I haven't any photos with me."

He jumped up and rushed to his briefcase. After rooting around in it, he yanked out a glossy sheet and handed it to her.

It was a black-and-white still from *Injury*. Dani had an FBI badge pinned to the lapel of her designer suit and aimed a gun toward the camera. Her hair framed her face in a dark halo, and her lips curled into a sly smile.

"I'd be happy to sign this. To whom should I address it?"

Vega gave her a face-splitting grin. "Aaron."

CHAPTER 7

The driver slammed the door, shutting Dani into the limo's dim light and air conditioning. She opened her carry-on bag, which she'd insisted on hanging onto when he'd stowed her luggage, and pulled out a bottle of vodka.

What a hellish four days it had been. She was glad to be back in the States, back in LA. Almost breaking a nail in the attempt, she struggled the wrapper off the top of the bottle. Fingers shaking, she pried up the plastic-topped cork stopper and tried not to spill while she poured it into a martini glass she found in the limo's bar.

She glanced out the window and realized the car was heading to the freeway, back to her apartment. Why not? The driver would've been instructed to do just that, and it made sense she'd want to head home after a trip out of the country.

She slid down the panel that separated them while trying to remember his name. *Cope. Yeah, that's it.* Short for Copeland, but he preferred just "Cope." Dani couldn't remember his first name. "Cope, I don't want to go home."

"Where would you like to go, Miss?"

"Somewhere I can get some air and no one will harass me. Do you know anyplace like that?"

"Sure. It's a long drive, but it's a nice view. I go there sometimes to get away. Will that be acceptable?"

"All right."

"I'll let Mr. Madden know."

Dani frowned and gulped her warm, Sahara-dry martini. "John asked you to call him when I was in the car." It wasn't a question. There was a time when she'd have found John's controlling nature comforting.

"He wants to make sure you arrived okay."

"Yeah, and he wants to make sure I go home and not to a bar." Dani held up her drink so Cope could see it in the rear-view mirror. "Cheers."

He nodded but didn't speak—not to her, anyway. He used the voice-recognition on the limo phone to call John. The conversation was brief. Dani could tell John was happy to hear she was back safe and sound, but suspicious that she wasn't heading straight home. Cope assured him they weren't heading to a bar and didn't rat her out about the martini.

They drove in silence for an hour, Dani sipping her way through three martinis. By the time Cope parked the car, she was flying high and tipsy enough to have wiped out the memory of the visit to her mother in prison. It had been a painful disaster, and, in her mind, the meeting with Detective Aaron Vega had been unproductive. Worse yet, for the last three nights, the same nightmare had haunted her and made her terrified to go to sleep.

In the dream, Dani is five years old and alone in her room. Lilli storms in as she did many times over the years Dani lived with her.

Lilli grabs Dani's arm and shrieks, "I'll bury you." Her mother stuffs Dani into a coffin, slamming the lid closed, locking her inside the satin-lined box.

When, in the dream, clods of earth hit the top of the coffin, Dani's consciousness would kick in. She'd realize she was being buried alive and startle awake, drenched in sweat and stifling a scream.

That dream killed her sleep no matter what time of night or early morning she woke from it. As a result, she'd had only ten hours sleep over four days.

Aware the car had stopped, Dani glanced up when Cope opened the door and offered her his hand. She took it, stepped out onto dirt, and immediately regretted her choice of footwear.

Her spike-heeled sandals—no, her *come fuck me shoes*—would be a problem on the soft earth of the cliffs ahead. Dani swayed and tossed her empty martini glass back into the car. It landed on the seat and bounced off. Through an alcohol fog, she noticed it didn't break.

Cope put one hand under her arm and the other around her shoulder. "Not the best idea to bring you here."

She giggled though she found nothing in her situation funny. "Shit. We're here. Let's go for a walk. I'll take off the stupid shoes."

He eased her back into the car, and she slipped off her heels. He leaned across her and took a bottle of water out of the bar fridge, uncapped it, took a swig, and handed it to her. "Your turn."

Dutifully she chugged some water. She could feel it going down, and it struck her then she hadn't eaten that day. She braced for the coming attempt at standing.

Cope gripped her arms and helped her up. The car door slammed shut behind her, and he locked the limo.

"Wait." She put a hand on his arm. "Leave your cell phone here."

"I can't do that, Miss Grayson. I need to stay in contact with dispatch."

"Please? I need quiet, and I don't want anyone to know where I am."

"It's on vibrate."

"I'd rather you turned it off. You can check for messages. Will that be okay?"

He agreed, reluctantly, turned off the cell phone, and clipped it to his belt.

Dani gazed around. They stood on a field that stretched out twenty feet in front of them, ending at the edge of a cliff. She heard the ocean below. Behind them, the road, lined with palm trees, branched off in two directions. In the distance stood a large, white house.

"Where are we?" The place looked somewhat familiar. Had she partied around here before?

"My parents' place is over there." Cope motioned toward the house in the distance. "It's quiet here. Private. No one will bug you. It's the one place that won't be crawling with paparazzi. We can walk to the beach using the trail along the side."

He led her to a dirt path, and they followed it, Cope guiding her steps and supporting her.

"You live there?" She was surprised. That place was worth millions.

"No. I have an apartment in Pacific Palisades."

She arched her brows. That wouldn't be cheap either. It was where her apartment was. "On a chauffeur's wage, or do Mom and Dad give you a hand?"

Cope pressed his lips together in a tight line, and his eyes narrowed. Maybe she'd struck a nerve. "I'm sorry. That was rude." She took another sip of the water.

"It's okay." He sighed. "Yes, they helped me out with the down payment. But I'm saving to start my own limo service soon."

"How old are you?"

He looked away, and just as she thought he wouldn't answer, he said, "Twenty-eight."

Three years older than she was.

He pointed to the bottom of the trail, which ended in a rocky scree, and beyond that, the beach. "That'll be hard on your feet. I'll carry you over it, if that's okay."

She nodded and slid her arms around his neck. He lifted her effortlessly, and she leaned her head on his shoulder, relieved to stop walking. He picked his way across the rocks, and she molded to his chest, fatigue making her eyelids droop. He smelled of fresh air and a hint of spicy soap, and she breathed it in, finding it comforting.

When he set her on the sand, she stumbled. He gripped her arm again and steered her toward the shoreline. "The sand's not too hot on your feet, I hope. I didn't think this through."

She shook her head. "It's warmer than I'd like, but not burning." She chugged more water. Suddenly, she had enough of being drunk and wanted to wash the alcohol out of her system.

The strong, salty breeze refreshed her.

"This is wonderful." She sucked deep gulps of sea air into her lungs. Dani let go of Cope and faced the setting sun. Eyes closed, she absorbed the warmth and light. The sound of seagulls crying and ocean waves crashing on the shore soothed her. She opened her eyes and caught him staring.

He grinned, which made him look boyish. He removed his jacket and set it on the sand. "Have a seat."

She shook her head. "Your jacket."

He stared at her, puzzled. "It'll dry clean."

She sat, looking out over the ocean, avoiding his eyes. What must he think of her?

"How long have you been driving me around, Cope?"

"Three months this time, Miss Grayson." He was always polite, deferential. "Though I sometimes drove for you before that."

She couldn't believe she knew nothing about the man who'd been driving her around so long. Granted, John had done the hiring, but she'd always treated Cope like a servant. She hadn't thought about him having a personal life independent of chauffeuring her around.

He'd always been there when required, followed her instructions, and looked after her when she needed it, which was more often than she cared to admit. He always made sure she arrived home safe, no matter how drunk she was, or how late the party ended or bar closed.

"Call me Dani. Miss Grayson sounds so formal." She smiled at him, and he smiled back.

Now that his jacket was off, she took a long, lingering look at his chest and noticed the muscles under his shirt. His chestnut hair, deep brown eyes, nice lips, and ripped bod made him a great package—too bad he wasn't older.

She put her head in her hands.

Knock it off, Dani. He's your fucking driver. That reminder made her relax. She didn't have to be on with him. He'd seen her puking drunk—more than once. She patted the spot next to her. "Please, sit with me? I promise to behave."

He sat, partly on the jacket, partly on the sand.

The sun hovered near the horizon. There was a pleasant mix of lingering warmth from the setting sun and body heat from the man next to her. Dani sipped her water and let peace infuse her.

32

They sat together, talking about nothing important, just enjoying the fresh, cool air and the soothing atmosphere, while the sun sank lower beyond the edge of the ocean.

Intimacy claimed Dani, and she reveled in it. "Tell me about yourself, Cope. Where did you go to school?"

He told her about his years at college, and she listened, envying him the ability to live a normal life. His parents sounded demanding, but in a way that Dani thought showed they cared though he said he resented their intrusions into his decisions.

"No one ever told me how to run my life. My mother ..." She choked on the words and shook her head, unable to continue.

"It's okay, Dani," Cope said. He put an arm around her, and she leaned into him relishing the touch.

Commotion from above made them both look toward the limo parked at the top of the bluffs. A man and woman in security uniforms picked their way along the steep incline down which Cope had carried her. He leapt up and went to meet them. Dani's heart sank. The couple was from the limo service, and the anger on their faces was directed at Cope.

CHAPTER 8

Unable to hear what the newcomers said to Cope, Dani stood and swished through the sand toward them. Raised voices swept by on the wind, garbled and unintelligible. She quickened her pace and finally got close enough.

"I have my cell phone. It's off." He removed the phone from the clip on his belt and turned it on. A series of staccato beeps heralded the incoming messages.

The man, a hulking giant who looked like his uniform might burst at the seams if he exerted himself too much, frowned. "Call in, Cope. We're glad you're both safe, but this won't go well. You went against company policy."

"I'm sorry. I was accommodating the client." He indicated Dani with a wave of his hand. "I meant to check my messages, but I forgot."

"Call it in." The woman's voice sounded less angry than the man's, but her tone was worried. "They're concerned and tracked you using the GPS on the car. It didn't look good that the car was parked at the top of a bluff and we couldn't reach either of you."

Cope called the office and talked to his supervisor. The explanation he gave sounded flimsy even to Dani, and he was silent while the man at the other end of the phone ranted, seemingly without taking a breath.

Face grim, Cope hung up the phone and turned to the security team. "You two can return to the office. I've been instructed to take Miss Grayson home, and I'll do that now."

"You okay, Cope? What did Newt say?" the woman asked.

"We'll talk later, Amanda." He touched the security officer's arm, lingering on it in a way that aroused a hint of irrational jealousy in Dani.

Amanda gave him a half-smile, reassuring, promising to see him later. Again Dani felt a little stab and wondered why it should bother her. She recalled his strong arms carrying her, the offer of his jacket to sit on, and intimacy that had grown between them. A stubborn desire to hang onto that jolted her, making her want him in way that felt strange and unfamiliar to her.

When security had left, Cope asked Dani to wait while he retrieved his jacket from the shore. He walked down while she watched, squinting in the fading light. He moved like an athlete, and when he bent over to pick up his jacket, she ogled his ass, glad he couldn't see her.

Back in the limo, Dani opened another bottle of water and took a swig while Cope tossed his jacket into the front passenger seat and climbed into the car.

"I'm sorry, Cope. It's my fault. I'll explain everything and make sure they know you're not to blame."

"Don't worry about it, Miss. It was my choice to turn off the phone, and my neglect that kept it off."

Was it wrong that it hurt he referred to her as Miss? Under the circumstances, she didn't blame him, but wanted him to say her name again. *Next time, I'll correct him.*

When he took her home, he walked her up to her apartment unit, carrying her bags. They said good night, and before he walked away, Dani learned his first name was Robert.

***

"They fired him?" Dani couldn't believe what John had just said. "What do you mean they fired him? It was my fault. Why are they punishing him?" Hot anger making her restless, she paced the living room between the couch and the loveseat and then circled the coffee table. "God dammit, John, Cope needs that job."

"I'm sorry. I have no control over that. Copeland deserved a reprimand. The man went against policy. Do you have any idea the panic we were in when we couldn't reach either of you? Then they located the car parked on the bluffs by the ocean? I was afraid you'd been kidnapped and your driver was at the bottom of the sea with a bullet in his head and cement shoes on his feet."

"That's very imaginative. You should write novels. He checked in with you when he picked me up from the airport. He told you I wasn't going home. What more do you want?"

A frustrated sigh told her John was reaching the end of his patience. "You feel responsible for what happened. I get that. And yes, he told me you were going for a drive. Next thing I know, you're unreachable and the car is out in the middle of nowhere."

"At his parents' place."

"I didn't have time to check the deed on the property, Dani. I'm glad you were both fine, but that's where the problem arises. Copeland shirked his responsibility, and you're an important client. That's the end of it. He's out."

Dani disconnected the call and tried the limo company. At first, the owner, Dale Newton, or Newt, as his employees called him, tried to placate her. His voice sounded reasonable, as if she was missing the point but would soon get up to speed. When she refused to accept his decision as final, an edge crept into his voice, and he sputtered at her until she wanted to slam the phone down.

"Newt," she interrupted. "I don't want anyone else to drive me. Get him back." She paced again, faster, covering the hallway, the living room, drifting around the bedrooms. The thought of losing Cope, of not seeing him every day, though she'd taken him for granted for months, put her in a panic.

"You can't fire him. It's not his fault. I told him to turn off the phone, and I distracted him from checking in. It won't happen again. Please. Don't do this. He's a good driver, and he takes his job seriously."

When Newt spoke again, it sounded as if he was talking through gritted teeth. "The decision's final, Miss Grayson. Sorry. We gave him his papers, and he's gone. Your new driver has years of experience, and he's just as capable as Cope. You won't notice the difference. Don't blame yourself. He should know better than to allow a client, even an important one, to distract him."

"Fine. Just tell me where I can reach him."

"I'm sorry, but I can't give out personal information. Be aware, though, that you're fighting harder for his job than he did. He'll find something else. Don't worry about Cope."

"It's me, Newt, not a stranger asking for his phone number. I'm sure he won't mind. I'd have asked for it from him yesterday if I'd known you'd fire him. Please, give it to me so I can call him and apologize."

"I'm sorry, Miss Grayson. It's against—"

Dani pressed "End" as forcefully as her thumb could manage, cutting Newt off, but getting no satisfaction from it. Luanne. Luanne could track down Cope.

The assistant picked up on the first ring, and Dani didn't even have to disconnect before Luanne had somehow located a phone number.

"Thanks, Lu. You're a life saver." Dani entered the number into her phone, disconnected from Luanne, and called him.

The suggestion to lend him money was barely out of her mouth when he turned her down flat. Dani no longer paced the apartment. She'd curled up on the sofa, but now sat bolt upright, wondering if he'd lost his mind.

"What do you mean, 'no thank you?' "

"I mean, it's okay. You don't need to lend me money. I've already turned down my parents. I'll do this myself."

"It's just a loan. It's my fault you lost your job. Let me make it up to you. At least meet me for lunch, and we'll talk about it."

"I'm busy. Maybe another time. I'm putting together business proposals and meeting with investors. When I'm up and running, I'll call you. Don't worry about it; Newt was right to fire me. I'd have done the same with any driver who pulled what I did. It was negligent. I've learned my lesson."

"Listen, I own an investment company. I had to do something with my earnings, so I invest in start-up companies. They'll look at your proposal. Consider it good networking."

"No, I don't want to owe you, and I don't want people to think I used you for your money."

"No one will think that. I want to help you."

"Thank you, but I'll be fine. Take care, Dani." The line clicked, and he was gone.

She leaned back against the cushions, considering what to do. At least he'd called her "Dani" and not "Miss." There had to be a way to help him.

An idea struck her, and she called Luanne. "Call Star Power Investments and tell William to call me. I want to talk to him about Robert Copeland."

Luanne promised to make the call, and Dani hung up the phone. One way or the other, she'd lend that money to Cope, even if he didn't know the money came from her. William Haz, the president of her investment company, could help with that.

The alarm sounded on her cell phone, alerting her it was time to leave for the meeting with the film studio. Happy with her scheme, Dani loaded a copy of the script for the new movie into a faux-leather bag and headed out the door.

CHAPTER 9

The limo pulled up to the building on the studio lot that housed the administrative offices for Danger Play. Dani waited for Mark, the new driver, to open her door, and then stepped out into the sultry afternoon heat. Four-inch heels making her taller than Mark, Dani looked him in the eyes and smiled at him, letting him take her hand to help steady her.

She walked through the revolving doors and into the lobby. The receptionist greeted Dani by name, smiling and making nice. The employees here were always welcoming and cheerful, but professional. They didn't act star-struck, and Dani appreciated that.

When she reached the conference room on the tenth floor, she noted that Greg Henderson wasn't there. She threw a puzzled glance at the executives, who sat across the room on the other side of the large round table. Danger Play's three owners, the film's producers, sat clustered together. The two men and one woman stood when she entered.

"Welcome, Dani. Good to be working with you again," Priscilla Houston said.

Dani clasped the hand the woman offered and shook it. Ten years older than Dani, Priscilla oozed confidence, the hand holding Dani's firm and smooth. Dani had enjoyed working on *Injury* and learning from Priscilla how to maneuver her way around a male-dominated world. Priscilla had even helped Dani extricate herself from the relationship with Greg when it went south. On the heels of that thought came the realization of the reason behind Greg's absence.

"Thank you. Nice to see you again." Dani shook hands with the two men, Kevin Patterson and Jack Kellerman. In their early fifties, both looked like they indulged in everything that could be considered an indulgence. Kevin's slight tan might signal liver damage rather than sun worship. She didn't think he'd looked that tan before, though this was California, the land of sun and sand.

They motioned her to sit, and she took a chair next to Priscilla. Jack got right to the point. "We wanted to speak to you in private. John mentioned to us that your prior relationship with Henderson made you hesitate accepting this contract. The first we heard of this was after you'd signed onto the picture. We're worried that problems between you and Greg might jeopardize scheduling. If you had concerns about working with him, why didn't you bring this to our attention before signing on?"

"It won't be an issue. I'm able to leave my personal life off the camera. When shooting starts, I'll be Felicity Sanderson, not Daniella Grayson. Felicity loves Charles Boyle, and that's who Greg will be. I signed because I don't see a problem here."

The executives exchanged glances, and Kevin spoke next. "What about Henderson? How's he feel about this?"

"Did he sign a contract with you?"

"Yes."

"Did he say he had any issues about working with me on this project?"

"No." Kevin raised his brows, looking progressively more amused as she continued firing questions at him.

"Did you talk to Greg at all about working with me?"

"No, Dani. We came to you first to ensure the star who's carrying the picture can perform when we need her to."

"Then relax because I'll be fine. Pris, you helped me during the last picture. You knew the problems Greg and I were having by the time the filming wrapped and the tour started. You traveled with us on some of those junkets. Did I let my personal life seep out into the public view?" Dani gazed into Priscilla's eyes.

"No, though the two of you made us nervous, and, as I recall, were hauled into the office for a reality check," she said. "That was then. Now, we want to hash things out before filming starts. The contracts have been signed, but if we thought you two couldn't work together, we'd tear up at least one of them—both if necessary. This is a business. It doesn't matter how much the public wants a sequel. Without you and Greg on board, I don't think it'll work, and funding it would be a waste of our money."

Priscilla threw a pointed glance at Kevin, then turned back to Dani. "Others might have a different opinion about whether it could go forward with one of you missing, but I think we need you both. That's why we had to be sure you can work with him, particularly the love scenes."

The sound of a man clearing his throat made them look up. John stood just inside the door, watching them. Zeroing in on Kevin, he said, "You ganged up on my client?"

"Not at all," Jack replied. Priscilla and Kevin remained silent. Jack continued. "We had to talk to her in private, feel her out about the Greg

Henderson situation."

"What situation?" The voice floated in from the hallway, and Henderson followed it in.

"Your messy breakup. Nothing personal," Jack said. "All is well, according to Dani, so now we discuss the schedule for the next few months. If everything goes smoothly, the preliminaries will be completed in a few weeks, and filming will start right after. Do you have your scripts with you?"

Dani reached into her bag and pulled out the large manila envelope containing the script to *Injury: Band-Aid Solution*. She looked Greg directly in his blazing blue eyes, purged the repulsion out of her soul, and said, "Shall we get started, Mr. Boyle?"

***

After the meeting, Dani stuffed her notes and script into her bag and said her goodbyes the moment John indicated he was leaving.

"Walk with me, John." She linked arms with him and steered him into the hallway. Aware that Henderson's gaze followed the two of them out the door, she moved as quickly as she could, considering her four-inch heels.

"Greg, wait, I want to talk to you." When Kevin spoke, Dani glanced over at Henderson, who stood stuffing his things back into his briefcase, face anxious.

He wants to talk. Grateful for Kevin's intervention, she picked up the pace, tugging John away from the conference room.

John waited until they were at the elevator before speaking. "I have a bad feeling about this. You shouldn't have told them everything was fine."

"What's wrong?"

"You know what's wrong. I see the way Henderson looks at you. Tell me what happened between you two. Why'd you leave him? Did he hit you?"

Dani managed not to flinch or give any sign John had guessed part of the truth. "We're okay. I won't date him. We're filming a movie together, and we're both professionals."

"You are, but I've seen Henderson on multiple benders during a shoot. I'm hoping their handlers stay on top of it and keep him sober. He showed up drunk more than once on *Injury* and dragged you down with him by the end of it. You're lucky you got away with your life. For Christ's sake, you ended up in *rehab addicted to coke.*"

"Don't worry. I'm not getting involved with him. How many times do I have to tell you?"

"As many times as needed to remind you not to get involved with him."

"Okay—" She stopped. She'd almost said "Dad"—joking, of course, but it wasn't funny to her anymore. Dani sighed.

John pressed the button to summon the elevator and said, "I hear Cope is shopping around a business proposal for a new limo company."

The mention of Cope's name brought with it a stab of guilt and a longing to see him. "He told me that, yes. I wanted to lend him the money, but he refused."

"Too bad. I was sorry he got fired. That would be one way to make up for it."

The elevator doors opened, and the pair stepped inside. As the doors closed, she spotted Henderson rushing from the conference room. Dani pretended not to see him, and the doors whisked shut.

"I've got something in the works," she said as she pressed 'G.'

"What's that?"

"Nothing I want to talk about yet, but I'm hoping it'll get Star Power on Cope's radar. I'm a silent partner, so he won't see I'm involved at all. If he applies on his own, I can push through his proposal and get him an interview. After that, it's up to him."

CHAPTER 10

Back in the limo, Dani checked for messages and found one from Cynthia, Will Haz's assistant. She called Star Power without listening to the message, and Cynthia put her through to the company president.

"Dani, how are you? Good to hear your voice. We haven't seen much of you at the office lately."

"I've been busy. Thank you for the flowers and the card you sent after the news about my father broke. That was sweet."

Will was thoughtful and a shrewd investor. She was grateful she'd found the perfect partner to run the company.

"You're welcome. Copeland submitted a proposal to Star Power yesterday. It looks good. Honestly, if you hadn't asked me to watch for it, I still would've considered it worthy of a meeting."

"That's wonderful. Tell me when he's due to present. I'd like to observe."

Will agreed, they said their goodbyes, and Dani disconnected the call. Soon, Cope would have a company of his own to run. It felt great to help out a friend.

On impulse and a sudden desire to see her former driver again, Dani called him and asked him to meet her for lunch. When he cheerfully agreed, she found her heart beating faster with anticipation. She directed Mark to drive her home so she could get ready for the date.

***

Dani stepped into the dim, intimate dining room of Genius, the upscale restaurant she'd chosen for her lunch date with Cope. Outside, the paparazzi hovered with their cameras, but she didn't give them a second thought.

The maître d' approached and greeted her. "Welcome to Genius, Miss Grayson. Your party is waiting."

Dani smiled as he led her past full tables and occupied booths. Voices mingled in a soft buzz, and a whiff of spice and roasted meat made her stomach growl. The host guided her to a secluded, candle-lit table at the back of the restaurant.

Cope smiled when he saw her and stood. He took both her hands in his, and grazed each cheek with a kiss, sending a shiver down her spine.

She stepped back and eyed his gray suit, noting the perfect fit, the notched collar, and the navy tie. "You look great."

He flashed her a grin and pulled a chair out for her. "You look gorgeous yourself," he replied as she lowered into the seat. "Did you do that for me?"

"Did you dress up for me?" she teased back.

He rested a hand on her shoulder. "Of course. I want to make you fall madly in love with me."

They both laughed self-consciously, but when the hand left her shoulder, she instantly craved his touch again.

A waiter appeared to take the drink order. Cope's frown and troubled gaze tipped Dani to his concern about her drinking.

Without hesitation, she said, "Sparkling water, please."

"I'll have the same. A bottle of your best." He grinned at the waiter and eased back into his chair. "You okay, Dani?"

"Me?" She waved away his question. "I should ask you. What's happening? Have you found funding for your business?"

"I've got a few meetings lined up, and one of them will get me the money I need."

"Call me when you're up and running. I'll be your first client."

"I'd be honored."

They chatted until the server returned with their drinks, and Dani realized she'd forgotten to review the menu. Cope asked the man for more time, and they scoured the options.

Since filming on the new picture would start soon, Dani had doubled her daily exercise quota and planned her meals carefully. She went with the roasted pumpkin salad. Cope chose the salmon with roasted cauliflower, squash puree, and roasted apples and kale.

After the server left, she reached across the table and placed her hand over Cope's. Their gazes locked, and she licked her lips. "Thank you for the other night." She lowered her eyes. "You've always looked out for me, and I took you for granted. Newt shouldn't have fired you—I never expected that. I can get so full of myself. Please forgive me. I got used to doing whatever I want, breaking the rules when I want, and it cost you your job. Why aren't you furious with me?"

He turned her hand over and held it in one of his while a finger lightly traced circles around her sensitive palm. She stifled a gasp at the jolt the touch speared through her body.

"I disobeyed the rules. I didn't argue with you much, and you didn't know what a breach of protocol it was."

"Yeah, but I was so drunk I didn't care, which was selfish." She gave him her brightest smile. "Forgive me?"

"Always. Let's not talk about this anymore. It's all good. I consider it an opportunity. If it wasn't for that, I'd still be preparing to start my own business instead of getting into massive action. I should thank you for what you did." His answering smile spread warmth through her body.

The food arrived, and they ate in silence, Dani studying his face. She was more familiar with the back of his head from sitting behind him in the limo. He had the hint of a mustache and a light stubble on his face that gave him a classy bad-boy appearance. Young. He looked so young, but the attraction between them was evident even if he wasn't her usual type.

A buzz sounded, and Cope set his fork down to pick up his cell phone. "Sorry, I meant to put it on silent." He glanced at the call display, and his face lit up. "The investment company. The meeting's confirmed for three o'clock tomorrow afternoon."

Dani's cell chimed then, and she reached into the front pocket of her handbag to see who'd texted. Star Power. *Meeting with Robert Copeland tomorrow at 3:00 PM.* Dani smiled and switched the phone to silent.

CHAPTER 11

The meeting room in the Star Power headquarters building resembled a lounge in a country club rather than a typical meeting room, and the décor was first class. The interior designer Dani had hired to decorate it had done an exceptional job. Smaller tables with leather chairs were scattered around the room, with a larger table and chairs taking center stage. A fireplace with mantle dominated the west wall, and a wet bar filled the east.

Hidden near the ceiling in the rich mahogany walls were video cameras that allowed Dani to view the meeting from any angle. On her screen, Cope stood in front of the main table, laser pointer in hand. The presentation projected onto the monitor on the north wall behind him. He'd been talking for thirty minutes, and she followed along on the handout she'd had smuggled to her.

Sorry she couldn't participate in the meeting, Dani experienced a surge of pride for Cope. He carried himself well, speaking with confidence and presenting the data in an organized and logical manner. His figures looked good, though in that area, she relied on the five-person team sitting in the room evaluating Cope's presentation.

By the time he was taking questions, Dani was sure the team would get on board with the idea. They interrogated Cope, and he fielded the queries and comments without hesitation. Once, he paused to sip from the bottle of water sitting next to his briefcase, perhaps giving himself time to think, or perhaps for effect. To Dani, he came across as thoughtful and professional—and hot.

When Cope completed his dog and pony show, he thanked everyone in the room for giving him the opportunity to speak. With flourish, he presented them each with a $100 coupon toward hiring one of his limos. Dani couldn't help grinning. The man had flair.

After Cope left, Dani hurried out of her office to the elevator. Almost

45

dancing with excitement, she hopped on and pressed the button for the twelfth floor. The ride seemed to take forever, and when the doors opened, she raced down the hall.

The team sat huddled at the table, reviewing the proposal, notes, and charts Cope had left them.

"Well?"

The group looked up, and Sam, the accounting director, cleared his throat in that fussy way he had and spoke before anyone else could jump in. "He's saved a substantial down payment, and his five-year plan looks solid. I need to dig into the numbers a little further to verify, but I'm optimistic it's a good investment."

Will nodded agreement, and Sheila flashed a thumbs up. Nate, who usually kissed Will's ass, and who reminded Dani of a gnome, frowned and shook his head. "I don't know if I want to invest in a limo service. They're a dime-a-dozen in LA."

Everyone turned to stare at him.

Nate locked his gaze on Dani. "I know you have your reasons for backing this guy, but the city doesn't need another limo service. But he impressed me. If he comes up with something more viable, I'll back him."

"I think he persuaded us he'll distinguish himself from the herd. The added special services, such as combining limo driver and a bodyguard licensed to carry, will give him an edge." The speaker, Carla, a young, aggressive MBA who'd helped Dani start the investment company, was one of the more trusted advisors. Dani tended to agree with Carla's conclusions, sometimes to the chagrin of the others. But so far, the young woman's instincts hadn't disappointed the team.

"Verify the numbers, Sam, and if you're satisfied, draw up a contract and send it to his lawyer. I want this pushed through fast. Will?" Dani, brows raised, glanced at the president to confirm he was on board, and when he nodded, she thanked them for their time and dismissed everyone but William.

When the others were gone, Dani lowered herself into one of the seats at the table and cleared her throat before speaking. "I'm not trying to step on anyone's toes here. I wanted to make sure you're okay with this. If it isn't a sound proposal, then tell me, and we won't invest. My judgment may be clouded since I feel I owe him."

Demeanor neutral, Will remained silent for a moment, as though considering what to tell her.

"Say it. I don't want anyone pussyfooting around me."

"We're not." He sounded annoyed at the accusation.

She shook her head. "I'm sorry. I didn't mean to imply you'd just tell me what I want to hear. You haven't yet. We leave that shit to Nate."

Will grinned at that.

She continued. "I've needed this investment business. It keeps me sane. In the two years since we started, it's done well. We're making good returns, and I owe that to this team. I didn't have much business sense—just a vision to help startups, provide opportunities people otherwise might never have. If others hadn't done that for me, I wouldn't be where I am. I was a nobody before, running from an abusive home. It could have gone any number of ways, all ending badly."

She sighed. "Sorry. I know Cope's not downtrodden. He comes from a wealthy family. But he's struggling to make it on his own, and I respect that."

"All right," Will said. "Is there a 'but?' "

A genuine smile of affection lit up her face. "*But* I won't put money on a losing proposition no matter who it is. I think his proposal is sound. The rest of you, except, oddly enough, Nate, seem to agree. Is that your assessment?"

"Yes. Don't worry about Nate. There might be something personal there, too. I think Nate has a connection to Cope's father—they call the father Big Cope. From what I understand, Nate and Big Cope used to be tight. Then something happened, and they no longer speak to each other."

That explained why Nate had the balls to disagree with the president when usually he was up Will's ass. Dani didn't like Nate, personally, but Will and Sam had insisted he was a valuable part of the team. He had as big a head for business as Carla but years more experience.

"Okay. As long as we're in agreement, I'll be comfortable backing him, and that's what I was hoping would happen. I don't want Cope to know of my involvement in this."

"If his lawyer does his due diligence, he'll find out you own this company sooner or later."

"I'll tell him myself before that happens. Cope didn't want me to lend him the money because he wanted to get the funding on his own. He's done that. It's just a coincidence it's my company backing him." But the uneasiness in her belly increased, and she doubted what she was saying.

***

"Scotch?" Margaret Copeland raised her glass and saluted Cope, who'd rushed into the room.

He shook his head. "No thanks."

He set his briefcase next to the couch on which his mother sat and then leaned in and kissed her cheek. "The meeting went well. I think they'll lend me the money."

"I'm glad for your sake, but I wish you'd reconsider and let us partner with you. We should work together as a family."

"I won't have that discussion again, Mother. Where's Ben?" Cope had hoped his older brother would be around. Ben was a computer information systems specialist, and Cope wanted his advice on technology for his business.

"A meeting. I never see anyone around here during the day. You know Nate is part of the decision to lend you the money?"

"Yes. He was there when I presented. I'm not worried. If Star Power doesn't lend me the money, I'll find someone else. I've had meetings with two other investors, and they both went well."

"The cocktail party on Saturday will be at eight. I want you to bring a date."

"Sure." Maybe he'd ask Dani. He wasn't working for her anymore, and if he had to bring a date, he'd like to bring her.

"Katherine Bloomington is back from college, and I've always thought it would be nice if the two of you got together."

"No, thanks."

"What's wrong with Katherine? Are you seeing someone else?"

Cope sat at the opposite end of the couch and considered pouring himself that scotch. "I might be."

"Why haven't you mentioned it or brought her over? Who is she?"

"I'm not sure it's a thing yet. I've just started seeing her." Cope considered the lunch date at Genius their official first date, so it counted as seeing each other. If he didn't make sure his mother believed he was with someone, she'd push him to date Katherine. That was something Margaret had done before Katherine and Cope had gone off to college.

"What's her name?"

"Let me ask her if she can come first, and then I'll let you know who she is."

Margaret pursed her lips and frowned. "Is she not from a good family?"

Cope sighed. Good family, to his mother, meant another resident of billionaires' row. He was sure Dani wouldn't pass Margaret's pedigree test, but he didn't care. Even if things didn't work out between them, he wanted to give it a shot and refused to let his mother spoil it.

He glanced at the time: five-forty. He stood, picked up his briefcase, and gave Margaret another peck on the cheek. "I'll see you Saturday. I've got to run."

"You just got here, Robert. Where are you going now?"

"Dinner plans." Before she could ask any more questions, he raced out the door.

CHAPTER 12

Dani hurried from the Star Power building to the limo. Guilt squeezed her when Mark opened the door for her. His days as her driver were numbered. As soon as Cope's company was up and running, she'd give her business to him.

Seated in the back of the car, Dani opened the bar, but reached for the bottle of water instead of the alcohol without hesitation. Life was too full and busy to dull it with alcohol.

Her cell phone buzzed. She checked the call display. A text from Cope: *Great meeting. Maybe too optimistic, but let's celebrate. My treat.*

Excited at the prospect of seeing him again so soon, Dani texted back: *Where would you like to meet?*

Come to my place. I'll make dinner.

She bit her lip, and a thrill ran through her belly. *I'd love that. What's your address?*

When he sent the information, she asked him to give her two hours, and instructed Mark to take her home.

Back in her apartment, after a quick shower, she considered what to wear. Cope had become important to her—more than a friend, and she wanted something classy yet sexy.

A black sheath dress caught her eye. It would hug her figure but wasn't slutty. She paired it with black heels, two inches—lower than her usual four-inch heels—she wanted comfort tonight. A platinum and diamond sapphire bracelet and opal ring from her jewelry box accessorized the ensemble. She dressed, fixed her hair, and did her makeup while thinking about the evening ahead.

She'd tell Cope tonight it was her investment firm he'd presented at that day. Better he find out from her than anyone else. If he hated the idea that much, he'd be able to back out of any proposed deal before signing a contract.

Ready, she hunted for her purse and found it on the end of her bed. She grabbed it and transferred her wallet and other essentials to a black, faux-leather clutch that matched her shoes.

Thirty minutes later, she stood at the door of Cope's apartment unit with a bottle of sparkling mineral water under her arm. When he opened the door, her breath caught at the sight of him. He wore a white dress shirt, open at the collar, no tie, and black dress pants that hugged his hips. She handed him the bottle and melted when he grinned in that happy-boy way he had that lit up his eyes.

"Come in." He stepped back into the foyer and held the door open for her.

Dani entered a modestly furnished apartment, small and cozy. Delighted to be in his space, she raised up on tiptoes to plant a kiss on his cheek. "Thanks for the invite. I'm so happy you called me over."

"Want a tour? It's not much, but I'm proud of it." Cope swept his arm around the room, encompassing the living room, dining room, and kitchen, and grinned. "That's most of it."

He set the bottle on the kitchen counter as they walked by and led her into his bedroom. Her gaze diverted to the bed, which took up most of the tiny bedroom, she had an urge to grab him and pull him onto it.

Control yourself, crazy lady. Be classy. She almost laughed out loud as an image of her staggering drunk on the beach flashed through her mind. He'd seen her puking up alcohol more than once. Classy was already off the table.

What was she doing here, in her dress-up clothes and fancy hair and makeup? The prolonged silence made her glance at him. He stared at her, puzzled, expectant.

"You've seen me at my worst. I don't know what you think of me or how to act around you."

"You're nervous?" He said it as if he was curious, not surprised.

She nodded. "If I were you, I wouldn't like me very much."

He stepped to her side. His arms went around her, and his mouth covered hers. He pressed her against his body, and she molded to him as though they were made to fit together.

A moan escaped her when his tongue darted into her mouth, hungry and insistent. The next moment, he released her, but had to grab her again when she swayed.

"I've been wanting to do that since the day we met. But you were my boss, and I had to keep it professional. After that, I've been looking for an opening. How could I not like you?" He stroked her face, pushing the stray strands of hair from her cheeks and forehead. "Because you had a tough time coping with everything? It was difficult to watch, Dani, but it wasn't your fault, and I did my best to protect you."

To her horror, she burst into tears.

"Dani?"

Sobs continued to tear out from deep in her chest. An attempt to speak failed.

He pressed her head against his shoulder, one hand stroking her hair.

"I barely acknowledged you. What a snob. How could you put up with me? Almost every night, you had to either drag or carry me up to my apartment. More than once, you helped me to the bathroom to puke. God, I'm so embarrassed."

He sighed. "I've had my share of nights like that—just perhaps not as many as you."

She jerked her head up, but saw he was smiling. Unable to resist, she smiled in return. "You're great at holding my hair back and never took advantage of me." The wonder in her voice rang in her ears, and she flushed. "I don't mean to imply you'd do that."

"It's okay. You were always this beautiful, fragile, vulnerable young woman, and I'd want to kill anyone who took advantage of that. The times you spent with Henderson were particularly grating. He used you, if you don't mind my opinion, but I couldn't interfere, because you chose to be with him."

Not wanting to discuss Henderson with Cope, she changed the subject. "What happens now? Between us, I mean?"

"What would you like to happen between us?"

"I like spending time with you?"

"Is that a question?" As if unaware he was doing it, he kissed the top of her head.

"No. It sounded like a question, but I know I like spending time with you. When we're not together, I miss you, and I want to hear your voice, tell you little things. Sometimes, I talk to you in my head because I want to tell you something and you're not there."

"I can fix that. I'd love to spend more time with you. My parents are having a party on Saturday night. Come with me."

Dani sucked in her breath. "To your parents' house?" What would his parents think of her? Never mind. She wanted to see him. If she didn't go with him, she'd spend Saturday night without him, and he'd ask someone else instead.

"Yes, I'd like that."

"Great. I'll pick you up around seven ..." He said it in a whisper and trailed off. He slid a hand under her chin and raised her mouth up to meet his. They kissed, light nibbles at first, then more insistent, demanding, each devouring the other.

The earth seemed to tilt when Cope lowered Dani backward onto the bed. With one hand, he captured first her right wrist, then the left, and raised her arms above her head. He stopped the kiss, and she gasped in protest.

"Do you want to keep going?"

She nodded, whimpered.

"Say it." His body draped half on her.

She pulled her wrists free and cupped his face with her hands. "Yes. I want to keep going. Don't you dare stop." A slight hiss emphasized the 's' in stop, the ache for him rising through her body.

He plunged his mouth back onto hers, lips and tongue working on her, tasting her. She moaned. She'd never wanted anyone the way she wanted Cope right now. The weight of his body on hers wasn't enough.

Fingers trembling, she plucked at the buttons on his shirt. He rolled to the side to give her room, and one of his hands brushed her thighs and slid under her dress.

His shirt peeled back to reveal a taut, muscular chest. With frantic movements, she stripped his torso, even though it meant pulling his hands from her body.

Freed from the shirt, he gripped the bottom of her dress, pulled it up and over her head, and tossed it to the floor. She kicked off her shoes while unbuckling his belt and came close to ripping the button off his pants in her frenzy.

"Take them off, now." Dani panted and tugged at the fly. "Don't make me beg."

A growl sounded from low in his throat, and he slid his pants and underwear off and hurled them to the floor. She slipped off her thong and with the distracting clothing out of the way, attacked his body with gusto.

"You're so fit." She loved the hard, smooth lines of his chest and arms and ran a hand along the curve of his ass.

Warm palms massaged and kneaded her breasts, her butt, and her thighs, moving, caressing, and leaving her breathless, while his mouth feasted on hers. She lost herself in him, savored his touch, which covered the gamut from tender and gentle to passionate and forceful.

When she was ready to take him into her, he put on a condom. She used her hand to guide him and wrapped her legs around his waist in a deep desire to be one with him.

"Ah, Daniella. Oh, God." The cries, soft, urgent, reverberated in her ear and stimulated her to move faster—meet force with more force.

"Robert. Oh, Robert." Need. She was need and nothing else. *Take me, please, just take me.* But she didn't say it out loud, willing him to know it. And to her delight, he did.

He made love to her in a way she'd never experienced. She responded to him, received his ardor, and absorbed it. Cries and moans escaped her lips.

She screamed in wild release when she climaxed, and he followed right after.

Eyes damp with tears from the unbearable poignancy of it, Dani struggled to contain her emotions.

Cope collapsed on her, and she stroked his back, an affectionate gesture she'd never made with anyone else.

How much intimacy had she missed with the random men who'd passed through her life? With John's associates, she'd been desperate for attention, spiteful, uncaring. She'd taken from them and gave nothing, though, they'd used her as much as she'd used them.

Most of the time, her hookups had been alcohol induced, as every time she'd made a play for John she'd been sauced. It wasn't an excuse and didn't justify throwing herself at a married man and expecting him to take the bait—it's just what had happened.

"You okay?" Cope kissed her cheek and ran a finger along her tear-damp temple. "You're crying?" Concern laced his voice, and he raised himself on an elbow.

"You'll laugh."

"Of course not. What's wrong? Did I do something?"

Dani pressed him to her body in a bear hug.

He exhaled, the breath forced from him when she squeezed her arms tight around his back. "You're stronger than you look. But you're not getting off that easy. Tell me; why the tears?"

"I feel moved, somehow, as if the intimacy was too much for me."

"Are you sorry?" He frowned, looked worried.

"Oh, God, no. I've never felt that close to someone while having sex. That's the thing. That's the first time I've made love instead of just fucking." She shivered, chilled.

"Let's climb under the blankets," he said.

He helped her snuggle under the covers, and she curled into the crook of his arm, laying her head on his chest. "Your body—so warm. It's heaven under here."

"Oh, damn. Dinner. There's a lasagna in the oven. That timer will go off soon." He glanced at the clock. "I was supposed to make the salad and garlic bread while it baked."

She laughed, carefree and happy. "It's not important. We'll get up when the buzzer goes off, take out the lasagna, and I'll help you make the other stuff. Did you really make a lasagna for little ole me?"

He grinned, and her heart melted. "Sure did."

"I didn't know you could cook."

"You might want to taste it before you decide I can."

A strand of her hair wrapped around his fingers, and he absently played with it. She stroked his cheek, rough with five o'clock shadow. She pressed her lips to the bristles, then poked her tongue out and teased him with the tip.

Cope groaned. "We won't get to dinner if you keep that up."

She giggled.

He rolled her off him and pinned her under his body. Instantly, the passion ignited again, and when he bent his head to kiss her lips, she moaned, stopping short of screaming.

When the buzzer went off, they didn't hear it.

CHAPTER 13

Dani checked the time. Henderson was ten minutes late. She sat in her dressing room, a trailer on the location set lot. He'd texted that he wanted to meet with her before they started the first day of shooting. If he didn't show up soon, they wouldn't talk, and there'd be no chance to hash out whatever he thought needed resolving.

At least the scene they were about to film wasn't one of the romantic ones. Her heart jackhammered in her chest at the prospect of seeing him alone for the first time. The anticipation was excruciating. It was so like him to keep her waiting. No doubt he was aware how much anxiety he was creating.

Footsteps approached, and there was a tap on the door. Her heart fluttered, and she swallowed, her dry throat clicking. She didn't get up, unsure if her legs would hold her up. A mental picture of herself falling to the floor in front of him made her cringe.

"Come in."

The door opened and Greg Henderson stepped inside. He looked like a golden god, the fucking asshole. Dani's breath caught in her throat. She forced herself to look away, feigning indifference, and picked up the bottle of water on her dressing table.

"Water? Or vodka in a water bottle?" Henderson didn't sound as if he was mocking her, but she wasn't sure.

She let it roll off her. "I'm not drinking. What do you want?"

"I didn't want our first time together to be on camera. That meeting at DP didn't count. You barely said two words to me."

The hurt behind the words stabbed at her, and she flinched.

Henderson continued, either not noticing or not caring. "I thought it might be difficult for you."

Again, she listened for mockery and found none. She let her gaze drift back to his body, then his face. He wore jeans, a plain black T-shirt, and a crooked smile. She'd always loved that smile.

He closed the door, and Dani gasped when he locked it. His presence stifled her, and she felt the air leave the room. Her hand trembled, and she had to set down the bottle of water.

"I was afraid you'd boycott the picture if I was involved." He tilted his head down and looked at her through half-lidded eyes.

I've never seen his humble side. Could be he's up to something.

He cleared his throat. "Thank you for that."

"If I'd forced them to choose between us, I suppose they might have picked me. But, let's be honest: the picture would suck without you, and the public wants us together—at least on screen, anyway."

"Maybe off screen, too, baby." He moved closer to her. "I've missed you."

"Stay away." She hadn't meant to sound so harsh, but his proximity was triggering memories she'd rather leave buried. She had a flash of herself face down on the floor, Henderson on his knees behind her, both of them naked and rutting like pigs.

She pushed it away.

He'd used her. He'd discarded her. Another surrogate father, though he'd been younger than the others—only ten years older than she was.

She licked dry lips.

He exhaled, loudly. "Baby, it makes me crazy when you do that."

"Go to hell. Do you really think you can come in here and pick up where you left off? Just because we're co-stars doesn't mean I'll let you use me again."

"I didn't use you."

"What else would you call it? You fucked me, and when your next picture started filming, you moved on to the next starlet. Typical. I don't know why I thought I'd be the exception. Oh, wait. Because you told me I was different—that I was the exception—that I was *the one*. You played me, you used me, and you cheated on me. I'm not interested in a fuck buddy for this movie."

"I didn't intend for things to get so out of control. Sorry, baby. That other girl meant nothing to me. We weren't even dating. Yes, we slept together during filming, but only after you blew up and threw me out."

"You hurt me, Greg—physically hurt me. You hit me. I had enough of that growing up."

"Jesus, Dani. How many times do I have to apologize for the same thing? It was an accident. I wasn't even aiming for you. You never let me explain. I'd never hit a woman—especially not you."

She hesitated. Closing her eyes, she recalled that night. They'd both been drinking. In those days, they'd hardly spent a sober moment together. They drank and they fucked. Sometimes they ate something.

Henderson had conned Dani into having a threesome with a waitress they'd met at the restaurant where they'd had a mostly liquid dinner. Dani couldn't control her jealousy after, and Henderson couldn't control his rage. He took a swing at her during their fight. Wasn't aiming for her?

She laughed and opened her eyes. "There wasn't anyone else in the room, Greg."

"I didn't mean to hit you. Sure, I was angry and wanted to hit something, but not you."

"Yet that's what you did. We're lucky that girl didn't go to the tabloids with the whole sordid story."

Henderson flinched and looked away. He was hiding something—she knew him well enough to see that.

"What did you do?" It hit her. "You paid her off?"

He nodded. "I had to make sure it didn't bite us in the ass."

Dani realized she was standing, but couldn't remember getting up. She'd almost taken a step toward him. She sighed. They were dynamite and poison together: explosive and toxic.

"We can't go back there." She didn't sound as convinced this time.

His handsome face and electric blue eyes drew her to him. She caught herself before the moan escaped and turned her back on him.

"Leave." She faced him again. "Please. We'll be okay on set. But I can't see you outside of work. Besides, I'm sort of seeing someone else."

"Who?"

"No one you know." As soon as the words left her lips, she remembered that wasn't true. How many times had Cope chauffeured her and Henderson around on one of their all-night benders? She winced when she thought about her past behavior, what Cope had borne witness to.

"Then it doesn't matter if you tell me his name."

"Sorry. I'd rather not say. We just started dating. If it's going somewhere, I don't want anyone to interfere." *I don't want you to interfere.* The unspoken words hung in the air between them.

"Babe, give us a chance. If you're not serious about this guy, then have dinner with me tonight. I'll take you somewhere private or back to my place. We'll have a romantic dinner and see where the mood takes us."

She shook her head. "You're not hearing me. I'm seeing someone. It's serious enough that I don't want to jeopardize it. Let it go. We ended badly, and we can't make that mistake again. Focus on the film. That's what's important."

He looked as if he intended to step toward her, but he turned away instead and unlocked the door. He put his hand on the doorknob though he didn't turn it.

"Sorry about your father. When I heard what happened, I wanted to call you, but didn't know if you'd want to hear from me."

"I saw the interview."

To her surprise, he blushed.

"Christ. That wasn't one of my most shining moments." Henderson dropped his hand from the doorknob and turned back to her. "Sorry, Dani. For everything." His expression told her he wanted to say more, but he shook his head, opened the door, and walked out.

She sighed, relieved, and didn't stop him.

CHAPTER 14

"Cut." The director, Jake Ferguson, stepped over to Dani and moved a lock of hair off her shoulder.

"When you turn around next time, keep the hair out of your face. Let's do this again." He returned to his chair, and when the actors took their marks, he called action.

Dani walked across the room, prop gun raised and aimed at the guy playing her brother. "I don't want to shoot you, Ralph. Get up slowly and step away from the body."

Ralph, kneeling on the floor next to the "corpse," rose to his feet and said, "It's not what it looks like."

"I think it's exactly what it looks like." Dani took a step back when Ralph turned toward her. "Stay where you are. Charles. In here."

Footsteps behind her alerted her to Henderson's presence, her cue to turn her head. She pivoted, but her hair slid onto her face again.

"Cut." Ferguson stood, but before he could come near her, Henderson stepped over and smoothed the hair aside, his finger brushing her cheek.

"Take a break," Ferguson said. "Someone get the stylist in here. I don't want hair dropping into her face every time she moves." Most of the time, the director talked around the actors, not to them, unless to give a curt command or instruction. It was his weird way of focusing on the story, Dani had learned.

At first, she'd felt hurt and worried that Ferguson disliked her, but when she saw it wasn't a slight, she found it reassuring. His directions were minimal, his conversation non-existent. It allowed her to immerse herself in her character.

The actors relaxed. The actress playing the victim remained on the ground, trying not to disturb her makeup or smear the fake blood. Dani sat on the sofa, and Henderson took a seat next to her.

Ralph—for the life of her Dani couldn't remember his real name—sat on the floor next to his victim, and the two chatted. Dani thought they might be sleeping together already, and filming had only started a week ago.

So far, Henderson had behaved, though Dani thought he acted too familiar with her sometimes. Perhaps it was because, in the film, they were lovers, and she could accept that. But other times, she worried that he was trying to winnow his way back into her personal life.

His knee rested against hers now, and she wondered if she should tell him to back off. Afraid to cause problems on set, she decided against it, and, as casually as she could, disconnected herself from him by crossing her legs.

"You avoiding me, babe?"

"Not more than usual. Don't call me babe. I'm not your babe."

"A little touchy, aren't you? I don't mean anything by it. You wouldn't take it so personally if you felt nothing for me." He leaned in close and lowered his voice. "Admit it, babe: you miss me as much as I miss you. Loverboy isn't cutting it in the bedroom. Am I right? I've spoiled you for other men, haven't I?"

She thought she caught a whiff of alcohol and looked him in the eyes. She squinted, trying to gauge if he was drunk. Henderson was behaving more arrogant than usual, and he was never a happy drunk. If he'd started drinking on the job, there'd be trouble. Sooner or later, he'd do something stupid and obnoxious, and it would cause problems. If she were lucky, the fallout would only affect him, but she suspected she could become collateral damage.

"Have you been drinking?" She kept her voice to a whisper.

"I had one shot before I came out to do the scene. I'm not drunk."

Uneasy, she wondered what else he might be taking.

The stylist arrived then, and Dani occupied herself with getting her hair fixed.

Henderson lounged beside her, legs stretched out in front, one arm draped across the back of the sofa behind her.

Back ramrod straight, she sat forward, away from the possessive reach of his arm, hoping he assumed she did it to make things easier for the stylist. Unable to resist commenting, Dani said, "You going to make this a regular thing?"

"The shot? Nah. What do you care? It's not affecting my work."

"It will if you keep doing it. Be professional. Don't drink on the job."

"You telling me what to do? Sorry, babe. You don't have that right." Now Henderson sat ramrod straight, casual air shattered.

"I'm trying to help you. Remember how the last picture ended? Both of us were drinking every day, you more than me. Please don't start that again. There'll be problems."

"Remember our love scene last time? It was fun to shoot, wasn't it? I watched it again last night and thought about us. Amazing, babe, truly amazing."

Dani shot a quick glance at the stylist, who bore a neutral expression. A consummate professional, she wouldn't react to anything the two stars said. She also didn't know quite what he meant when he referenced the sex scene from *Injury*.

Henderson and Dani were a couple then, and both had been drinking before filming, loosening themselves up for the kind of scene that typically made actors nervous.

The strategy had worked. They'd gotten so loose and unselfconscious the sex hadn't been simulated. When the director yelled action, the lovemaking was real, and they'd got it in one take. She was sure the entire onset crew had known the two stars were doing it in front of them.

The love scene for this film was scheduled for two weeks away, and Dani wondered how the hell they'd get through it.

CHAPTER 15

Dani gazed at herself in the full-length mirror on the inside of her closet door and tried to like what she saw. She'd already changed four times. This time, she wore a long, black cocktail dress, simple lines, elegant, with a plunging V-neck and a slit up the side. Dani chose a pair of cream, open-toed pumps and a cream clutch to go with it.

A glance at the time reminded her she'd better hurry. Cope would be here in twenty minutes, and she still had to do her hair and makeup. The butterflies in her stomach kept fluttering while she worked to complete the look. What if his family didn't like her? What if she embarrassed him? What if someone told him she owned Star Power?

Since the night at Cope's place, Dani had wanted to find an opportunity to tell him the company was hers, but the moment hadn't presented itself. She'd intended to tell him that evening, but his lovemaking had pushed all thoughts of business out of her head. Lips curling into a smile at the memory of it, she put the finishing touches on her makeup and then verified the hair straightener was hot enough to use.

With a deft hand, she ran her hair through the styling tool in minutes, and by the time the buzzer on the intercom sounded, Dani was ready to go.

Cope met her in the lobby and, offering her his arm, guided her to the car, an Audi.

"It's weird to see you driving something other than a limo." She smiled at him, and he returned it, eyes shining.

"I've gotten so used to driving the limo, it sometimes feels weird to me too. I'm hoping to be able to change this one up in a few years. But I can wait. I like this car." He opened the passenger door for her, and she slid into the seat, tucking her dress in around her legs.

Forty minutes later, Dani stared out the window and watched the coast slide by, aware they were almost at their destination and dreading it.

"Not nervous, are you?"

She turned away from the window and stared at him. "How do you do that?"

"Do what?" He glanced at her, brows raised.

"Guess my mood and figure out what I'm thinking."

Cope laughed, a deep chuckle that brought a smile to her face and made her relax enough to breathe normally again.

"My beauty, don't ever play poker." He chuckled again, and this time, she joined in.

"Okay. I'm nervous. I want to make a good impression."

He took her hand and squeezed it a moment before returning his hand to the steering wheel. "Don't worry. You're gorgeous, smart, talented, and charming. Just be you, and they'll love you."

"Will your whole family be there?"

"If you mean the siblings and the parents, then yes, they will. Don't worry. I'll help you through it."

He turned off the highway and in another fifteen minutes pulled into the long, winding drive that led to the mansion Dani had glimpsed that night on the beach.

A large fountain, lit up with white lights, sparkled in the midst of a cobblestone walkway along the front of the house. The ten-car garage loomed up, and the door to one of the bays slid open when Cope pressed a button inside the Audi. The car eased into the garage and he cut the engine.

She waited while he came around the vehicle and opened the door. Nerves at full throttle, she clung to his arm, afraid she'd trip walking up the stone staircase to the expansive marble-columned porch. The front door opened before they reached the top of the stairs, and a young woman, younger than Dani by about five years, stepped out.

"Bobby!" The woman rushed out and grabbed Cope in a bear hug, smiling bright brown eyes at Dani while she did. "Mom told me you were bringing a date. I'm Heather."

Heather offered Dani her hand, then pulled her in for a hug as soon as their hands clasped. "Oh, I'm so excited to see you. Bobby doesn't usually bring dates home. You must be special." Heather winked, and Dani grinned, unable to help herself.

"I'm Dani Grayson."

The young woman stepped back and did a double take. "Oh my God. Daniella Grayson. Bobby, you didn't tell me you were dating Daniella Grayson. I've got to tell Nichole. Oh, God, she'll pee herself. We've seen all your movies." Heather rushed back into the house.

Dani glanced at Cope and saw the indulgent smile.

"She's still kind of a kid. I choose to find her charming." He rested a hand on the small of her back and guided her inside.

She tossed her head back in his direction, lips curling up into a sly grin. "Bobby?"

"Only my kid sister gets away with that." He shot her a scowl that looked more comic than threatening.

An older woman entered the room, dark hair swept back in an elegant up-do. She wore a Grecian-style evening dress, in cream, and Dani wondered if the woman had deliberately tried to match the color of the stucco outside. To steel her nerves at meeting Cope's mother, Dani pretended she was Felicity Sanderson, cloaking herself in her character's self-confidence.

"Mother, meet Daniella Grayson. Dani, Margaret." Cope put an arm around Dani's waist.

Dani extended a hand to Margaret, who smiled through gritted teeth and clasped the hand in a moist, floppy grip.

"How charming. You're dating a movie star. What's it like, Daniella, to have strange men throwing themselves at your feet? You must never want for male companionship."

Unsure what to make of that remark, Dani managed a polite smile. "Nice to meet you, Margaret."

"Please, dear, call me Mrs. Copeland."

A warm flush crept up Dani's face despite her resolve to act confident and as Felicity-like as she could manage. No writers to provide her with dialog here, though, and she had trouble coming up with her own charming banter.

Cope's arm tightened around her, and she found that a comfort.

"Be nice, Mother. Dani's my guest."

"I don't know if you're aware, darling, but Katherine's here." Margaret spoke to Cope, but kept her gaze on Dani. "Robert and Katherine used to be quite close before they each went off to college. I think she was his first love."

Cope sighed, then looked relieved when he caught the eye of a strikingly handsome older man walking down the stairs toward the group. "Dad. Come and meet Dani, my girlfriend."

Dani didn't flinch though she came close. So she'd graduated from date to girlfriend. How did she feel about that? She gazed up at Cope's face and wanted to kiss him all over. Apparently she was okay with it.

Cope's father reached the trio, and he offered Dani his hand. She accepted it with a genuine smile and felt herself blush again when he raised her hand to his mouth and lightly kissed it.

"Rupert Copeland. Everyone calls me Big Cope. Nice to meet you. I've seen most of your movies. Robert's a lucky man."

"Shall we go to the party room?" Margaret interrupted. She spun on her heel and headed to a corridor on the left.

Big Cope released Dani's hand and motioned for them to follow. He led them into a banquet hall, decorated as though for a wedding reception. Instead of banquet tables, bar tables with bar stools ringed the room's perimeter. An enormous stone fireplace consumed the west wall, a pyramid of candles inside it providing ambience. A bar, manned by two bartenders, spanned the far wall. A band played in the southeast corner. Couples swirled and swayed on the dance floor in the middle of the room.

"What would you like to drink, dear?" Big Cope offered Dani his arm, and she linked her hand through it and smiled.

"Mineral water with lime will be fine, thank you." Worried he might find that insulting, she braced herself for a negative reaction, but it didn't come. She didn't want a drink tonight. Her guard would go down, and based on Margaret's reaction, Dani thought she'd need both brain and body unscrambled by alcohol.

"Robert, why don't you hunt up Dani that drink while I get to know her better?"

Cope gave her a reassuring smile and a quick squeeze around the waist, then headed toward the bar. Big Cope drew Dani toward a nearby table, and they sat, perching on the barstools.

"How did you meet my son?"

Surprised that Cope didn't talk to his family about the job, she leaned in so she didn't have to shout too much over the music. "He was my limo driver." She almost mentioned her role in getting him fired when it occurred to her Cope might not want her to discuss it. She'd have to be careful what she said and to whom she said it. To calm her nerves, she drew in a deep breath and smiled.

She chatted with Big Cope, mostly about his son, which made her like the younger Cope even more. Big Cope's tone and words betrayed his pride in his youngest son. The older Copeland confided to Dani that the family had argued that young Cope needed them to partner with him. But Big Cope was secretly delighted that his son had secured the funding on his own.

"When he called me with the news, I couldn't have been more proud." Big Cope's eyes shone, and his gaze wandered over toward the bar.

She followed the glance, uneasy that she still hadn't told Cope the money came from a company she owned. She'd tell him tomorrow for sure. He was coming over for dinner, and she'd tell him then. She had to. It was getting to the point where he'd be unable to back out of the deal without a lot of headaches. But tonight wasn't the time to dump that on him.

A frown crossed Dani's face when she noticed Cope continued to stand at the bar, drinks already in hand, and the reason for the holdup was a woman. The woman talking to him—who kept him talking—beamed at him, laughing and touching his shoulder in a familiar way. Blonde, thin, dressed elegantly in a long white evening gown with spaghetti straps and a corset that accentuated her cleavage, she tossed back her head, obviously flirting.

"Katherine Bloomington," Big Cope said, helpfully. "Friend of the family. Bobby and Kate grew up and went to school together."

Margaret joined the couple at the bar and embraced Katherine with enthusiasm. Dani turned away and focused on Big Cope, asking him about his business, though when he responded, she barely heard anything he said. A knot of anxiety twisted in her solar plexus. She smiled at all the right moments, even managed a giggle at something funny Big Cope said, and forced herself to avoid checking on the scene at the bar.

The first indication Cope had returned was the glass of mineral water and lime appearing in front of her on the table. Dani breathed a quick sigh of relief and glanced at him, mouth curling up in appreciation. The smile faltered, but then continued to spread out of stubborn pride, when she saw Katherine stood beside him, an arm around his shoulder.

"Katherine Bloomington," the blonde predator said.

"Daniella Grayson." Dani held her hand out, trying not to hiss and determined to squelch the jealousy flooding through her.

Katherine's arm slid from Cope's shoulders and the women shook hands. "I'm so thrilled to meet you. My condolences on your father's death. What you're going through must be difficult."

Cope shot a dagger look at Katherine, who ignored it. Surprised, and oddly enough, touched, Dani shook her head at Cope, and said, "Thank you. I'm managing."

It occurred to Dani that Katherine was the first stranger to talk to her about what had happened who wasn't trying to get a scoop or comment from her.

"I loved my dad, and it's been difficult to hear how he died. My mother will be in prison for a long time."

"You volunteer with abused children at Child Rescue." Katherine leaned in close. "My sister mans the phones for them, and she told me she's seen you around. Hillary."

Dani smiled, and her eyes widened. "Yes. I know Hillary. She's wonderful with the children who call in needing help. Bloomington. I didn't make the connection." It was hard to dislike Katherine. If she was anything like her sister, Dani could understand why Cope would be attracted to her and why Margaret would want to throw them together.

Cope put an arm around Dani's shoulders and leaned in close to whisper in her ear. "If you want to escape, let me know. We'll go for a walk and some fresh air."

He kissed her cheek, and she smiled up at him. Maybe the evening wouldn't be so bad after all. After a few sips of mineral water, Dani realized she needed to use the ladies' room, asked for directions, and excused herself. She headed out into the hallway and looked to the left, where Cope had told her a bathroom existed.

Though Dani was well off, she wasn't used to extravagant living, and walking into a house that had a ballroom and lavish, multi-stall bathrooms overwhelmed her. Cope lived in this. No, that wasn't true. He lived in a one-bedroom apartment and was happy about it.

She entered the bathroom and headed for a stall.

Later, as Dani stepped to the sink to wash her hands, Margaret entered the bathroom. The only other woman in the room dried her hands, patted her hair, and walked out.

"Mrs. Copeland. You have a beautiful home."

"Thank you, dear, but it won't help you." Margaret folded her arms across her chest and met Dani's gaze in the mirror.

"Excuse me?"

"Bobby might sow some wild oats with you, but now that Katherine's back, I'm sure he'll come to his senses. It's nothing personal—it's just that they've known each other for such a long time. Nice as I'm sure you are, you ought to know that his heart belongs to someone else."

"I'll take that under advisement." Dani washed her hands, trying to keep them steady. Margaret's cruelty stung, and all she wanted to do was escape.

"Your mother murdered your father. We want no part of people like that in this family. How much do you want?"

Her mouth dropping open, Dani gasped, and her eyes went wide. Silently, she turned off the water and picked up one of the cloth hand towels rolled up in the basket on the counter. When her hands were dry, she tossed the towel into the bin on the floor and faced Margaret.

CHAPTER 16

Dani took a deep breath and forced herself not to cry. "I don't understand. Robert and I are just dating. We enjoy each other's company. I don't want anything from him."

"How much money would ensure you leave Bobby's life and stay out? Surely, we can come to an arrangement."

"I don't need money." Horrified, Dani stepped around Margaret and tried to make a run for the door.

Margaret snagged Dani's arm, stopping her. Long fingernails dug into her flesh, making her wince.

"That hurts." All of it hurt, but she focused on the tight grip and sharp nails, because if she thought about the rest, she'd certainly cry.

"I want you to stop seeing my son. Do you understand? You're not good enough for him. I've read the magazines. You've been in rehab for drug addiction. Bobby's a good boy. You'll ruin him." Margaret's eyes flashed, and her lips curled back in a grimace.

"Let go. Please." Sorry she'd agreed to come to the party, all Dani wanted to do was go home. "Let go now, and I won't tell Robert you tried to bribe me. But understand one thing: you won't bully me. I refuse to stop seeing him. He's capable of making his own decisions about his love life."

Margaret's hand, the one not gripping Dani's arm, twitched, as if she were contemplating slapping the actress.

Feet planted on the floor, Dani prepared to defend herself. At the very least, she'd stop Margaret from hitting her—she'd had enough of that shit from her own mother.

The hand at Margaret's side stayed there, and the one burrowed into Dani's biceps released.

Dani ran from the room.

***

The doors to the party room were closed, and Dani took a moment to collect herself before tugging them open and stepping inside.

Cope still sat at the table with Big Cope and Katherine, but another couple had joined them. Dani made her way to the table and hooked her arm through Cope's.

He looked at her, smiling, but the smile vanished when he saw her face. "What's wrong?"

Shit. He could always read her, an ability he'd probably developed on the job trying to anticipate his client's needs.

"I could use that walk now." If she could escape the crowd for a while, she'd be able to deal with what had happened between her and Margaret.

"Sure." He hopped off the barstool and led her into the corridor.

They slipped outside onto the veranda, and Cope guided her along the side of the house to the back of the property. A cobblestone pathway meandered through massive, landscaped gardens accented with fountains, statues, and topiary. An outdoor kitchen and den surrounded the sunroom connected to the back of the house.

Dani forgot about everything as she took in the opulence and beauty of it. "This is amazing. Did your parents build this house?"

"They bought it from the original owners and added on. Most of what you see, my parents built. Let's go to the gazebo. It has a fabulous view of the ocean."

In silence, they made their way around the various flower gardens, the scent of rich soil and ocean air soothing Dani's frayed nerves. A few deep breaths helped ease the knot in her stomach, and the hurt and anger inside dissipated.

The gazebo perched on the top of a cliff overlooking the ocean. Cope helped her up the steps and steered her to a screened-in opening on the west side, which offered an unobstructed view of the ocean. Strategically placed lights illuminated a path to the shore.

Dani gasped at the sight of it. She faltered in her heels, which pinched her feet and made walking uncomfortable. Glad to see cushioned seating arranged so that the ocean view was the focal point, she sat down on a loveseat, drawing Cope down beside her.

"What happened to make you so sad? Did you get bad news?"

Not wanting to upset him by divulging what his mother had done, Dani leaned into him, resting her head on his chest. "I'm overwhelmed. Tired. There's been so much going on. I needed some air and space."

Cope's hand stroked her hair, comforting and sweet. She should tell him about her involvement in the investment firm. Before she opened her mouth to speak, she bit back the words. What if he got angry and turned to

Katherine? But the longer she kept it to herself, the worse it would be when he finally found out. A heartfelt wish to keep it secret forever surged through her, but she knew that wasn't realistic.

If Margaret ever found out, she'd be delighted to fill him in, and that would kill any prospects Dani and Cope's relationship had. But spilling it now would be the worst decision. He'd be angry, they'd argue, and he'd fall into Katherine's arms. The possible catastrophic outcomes flooded into Dani's head one after the other.

The soft, gentle touch of his hand on her hair slowed her racing heart and eased her anxiety. Cope touched a finger under her chin and tilted her face up so their gazes locked, and then he dipped to cover her lips with his.

A lust-filled sigh escaped her, and he reacted by kissing her more deeply, his tongue probing her mouth. Letting the moment and Cope take her, she returned the kiss. Fists gripping the back of his shirt, she clung to him, wanting to hide here in the dark forever.

It reminded her of the time they'd sat on the beach by the ocean, but this time, she was sober, and he was hers. His lips kissed a trail down her face, her throat, to the plunging neckline of her dress, and paused there, nibbling and tasting the bare skin.

"Did you bring me out here to seduce me?" she gasped.

"You make it sound like it'll take work." The devilish grin he had when he wanted to tease her had returned, making her heart hammer against her chest.

"No, it would be way too easy for you," she breathed back.

Cope unzipped his pants and pulled Dani into his lap, hiking the dress around her waist as he did.

"Ah, God. That low-cut dress, the slit up the side showing off one leg, has been killing me. I have to have you right now." He sounded fierce, almost feral. Every touch of his fingers sent sparks racing to her loins. Dani heard the sound of a condom wrapper tearing open and buried her face in his neck.

"What if someone finds us out here?"

"In another few seconds, I won't care if they film it and post it to the Internet." Cope fumbled in the darkness and then lifted her so she straddled him. That made her giggle, though nervousness competed with wanton desire, leaving her tense but still insane with lust.

He held her hips, and Dani removed her panties and impaled herself on him, letting out a cry when he met her with a light thrust. They ground against one another, and she wrapped her legs around his waist and her arms around his neck. Mouths pressed together as if they were resuscitating one another, they tumbled into a passionate rhythm.

For a second, Cope came up for air, and said, "Daniella, I can't keep my hands off your body."

Her hands skimmed over his muscles and his soft hair. Everything about him was a miracle. His scent intoxicated her, and his voice soothed her. Cope, solid under her, in her, filled her and completed her.

The ecstasy, when it flooded her, made her melt in his arms, and as she released, he spent himself inside her. Heartbeat to heartbeat, they clung together, inhaling sex and ocean breezes.

She snuggled in his lap while he helped her put herself back together. Margaret's threats and intimidations roared back into Dani's mind, shattering her peace. Possessively, she hugged him and gave him a frenzied kiss.

"Whoa, you'll get me revved up again. What brought that on?"

"Nothing," she said. "I don't want to let you go, Cope, and I need to touch you."

"Not a problem." He kissed her cheek and her forehead.

No matter what, she'd never let Margaret steal this man away for someone else. But the doubt refused to go away. How would she ever be able to tell him the truth?

Later that night, Dani wrenched out of a nightmare, shaking and chilled. The vision, this time of Margaret forcing her into the coffin and burying her alive, kept her awake until almost dawn.

CHAPTER 17

Candles lit, Dani stepped back from the dining room table and admired her handiwork. The aroma of roasted chicken filled the air, the salad was done and keeping chilled in the fridge, and the mashed potatoes stayed warm in the toaster oven. All she needed now was Cope to arrive.

Since the night two weeks ago when they'd first slept together, she'd seen him every few days, though to Dani, that wasn't often enough. An ache in her heart intensified whenever she thought about him. She missed him—his touch, the sound of his voice, his laugh, his gorgeous body— everything about him. And he made her feel safe and cherished, something she'd never had from anyone else.

The doorbell rang, and she rushed over and threw open the door.

"Flowers. How sweet. Thank you." She accepted the bouquet of red roses, blue daisies, and fresh green carnations from Cope and headed to the kitchen to get a vase.

He followed her, removing his blazer and dropping it on the couch as he walked by. "You opened the door awfully fast."

"I was so excited you were here that I leaped to open it." She looked up, the comment puzzling her.

"Maybe it's not my place, but you're a celebrity. It's risky for you not to look through the peephole first. Don't say you checked because you opened the door too fast to have taken the time to verify my identity."

She frowned. "I should have looked. You're right. But I was expecting you. You texted me you were on your way." Not slowing in her quest to get a vase, she opened a cupboard door under the sink and retrieved a large glass urn.

"Yes, but since you gave me the access code, and I didn't have to buzz to come up, you didn't know who was there. What if I'd been delayed and a crazed fan had got into the building? Actresses have been killed opening their doors to homicidal fans."

She set the flowers on the table, trimmed the ends, and turned to the sink to put water in the vase. "I can only recall one example, so the odds are with me, but it doesn't hurt to be cautious. I'll check next time. Okay?" She gave him her biggest, most reassuring smile, touched by his concern.

Cope moved to her side, put his arms around her waist, and nuzzled her neck.

She sighed, loving the affection, basking in the comfort he provided. *God, I'm falling in love.* That surprised her—she hadn't thought herself capable.

"I'm worried, Daniella. You're exposed. Photographers stalk you. This thing with your mother has kept your face in the newspapers, on TV, in the magazines. Now you're filming a sequel to an Oscar-winning movie, and you're at risk. Hire a driver from my company, starting next month. I'll be open for business then. The money's in the bank, and I've got everything lined up and ready to open the doors on the first of June. The driver will double as a bodyguard."

"Robert." She set the vase full of water on the counter and faced him. Ignoring the twinge of guilt about his funding, she jumped on the bodyguard comment. "A bodyguard? Why? I'm not royalty."

"You're my queen." He grinned, and his lips grazed hers.

Her body responding, Dani pressed her mouth over his and gave him a deep, soul-shattering kiss.

"Keep this up," he muttered against her mouth, "and we'll burn this dinner, too."

She pulled away and picked up the vase. "Not this time, my friend. I won't be distracted. We'll have the lovely, yet simple, dinner I prepared." She winked. "Then we'll take this party into the bedroom, because by then, I won't be able to keep my hands off you."

Bodyguard? Did she really need a bodyguard? She supposed the idea wasn't that crazy. Why argue over it when Cope was only concerned for her safety? Other than John, who was more like a big brother to her now, no one had worried about her or cared what she did. It was nice.

Flower food packet opened, Dani dumped the contents into the water in the vase and arranged the flowers. She set the whole thing in the center of the kitchen table. "They're so beautiful."

"Glad you like them. You okay with the bodyguard? I don't want you rebelling and causing the poor guy grief. I've been in his shoes—I know how stubborn you can be."

"Yes. It won't hurt me to have added protection." She thought about Henderson. He made her increasingly uneasy. The other day, he'd asked her why she hadn't admitted to him it was Cope she was dating.

Dani and Cope had been careful to avoid being seen canoodling in public, though after going to his parents' place yesterday, the news was getting out. But the tabloids hadn't yet got hold of that tidbit about her personal life, so Henderson hadn't heard it from the media. When she'd questioned him, he refused to say how he'd found out. And he'd been drinking again on set.

The timer buzzed, and Dani went to take the chicken out of the oven while Cope disposed of the debris from the flowers.

"The dining room table is already set," she said. "We just need to carry the food in."

"I'll help." He headed for the fridge. "What do you need?"

"Start with the salad and the bottle of sparkling water. There's also organic juice if you prefer, and I have a well-stocked bar, but I haven't touched it since filming started."

They set the table and settled down to the meal. Conversation flowed, Dani relaxing from Cope's easy, affable manner.

"This is great. I didn't know you could cook."

"It relaxes me. Yes, I can afford to hire someone to do it, but I've always cooked for myself. When I was still with my mom, I made the meals for both of us." She left it at that—discussing her crappy, non-existent childhood would just bum them both out.

"I want to take you out for a change, on a real date," he said. "We've hidden in our apartments too long, and a party at my parents' doesn't count."

"The media will be on it if we step out in public." Did it matter to Cope whether his picture got in the paper?

"Does that bother you?" he said.

She shrugged. "If you don't care that our relationship becomes public knowledge, then we can go out." Henderson popped into her head again then. *But Greg already knows who I'm seeing. He wouldn't care.* Still, that he'd see pictures of her and Cope together worried her, though she didn't understand why. She'd seen pictures of Henderson with a variety of women since shooting started, and she'd felt nothing.

"What's wrong? You're scowling." Cope stopped eating and set his fork down.

She forced her face to relax and smiled at him. "Nothing. I'm okay with letting the news get out if you are."

"I have nothing to hide."

"They'll pick us apart. Once it gets out, everything you do will be under the microscope. They'll dig into your past. Remember when Greg and I were together? I wasn't a household name then, but I became one overnight. The whole world got to hear that my father had abandoned the family when I was five." She fell silent, remembering the whole sordid time.

"Speaking of Henderson, I've tried to keep my mouth shut about that ape, but if he does anything inappropriate, tell me."

"It'll be fine. I've taken care of myself for a long time."

Cope took her hand and kissed it. "I know." His voice became gentle. "I'm just acting like the jealous boyfriend. He's your ex, and I'm trying not to think about the sex scenes you'll be doing."

"The love scenes will be more technical than romantic. There'll be a minimal set crew because filming that type of scene can make you nervous." And it was scheduled for the next day, a fact she refused to disclose to Cope right now—why make him worry? When it was over and done, she'd mention it was in the past, and he'd be able to relax, knowing they'd got through it without problems.

"I can imagine." He finished the last mouthful of food. "Want to plan something for this weekend?"

Dani's heart surged at the prospect of going on a normal date. She thought about it as they cleared the table and did the dishes. It all seemed so domestic. Was this what John and his wife had? No wonder he'd refused to jeopardize it. An image popped into her head of her and Cope in a home of their own, surrounded by kids, a dog, cats …

Her cell phone buzzed. "Sorry," she said. "I meant to shut that off."

When she fished it out of the purse sitting on the couch, the call display showed "Greg Henderson." She turned it to silent. Let him leave a message. This was her private time with her boyfriend. She smiled at Cope. "Nothing that can't wait. Would you like a coffee or tea?"

"Shouldn't there be an 'or me' on the end of that question because that's the option I choose." He whispered it, thick and husky.

"What about dessert?"

"I'm thinking about dessert." He strode to her and captured Dani in his arms. Mouth sinking to hers, he devoured, taking her breath away.

The familiar jolt of desire spread through her body, starting at her stomach and weakening her knees. Savored kisses; shared passion. She tumbled into the lust and found affection, gentleness, and even love. Afraid she loved him, and that it was possible he loved her back, she focused on the physical, trembling, moaning to his caress.

The world rocked, but it was just her feet going out from under her as Cope lifted her into his arms. "I'm taking you to the bedroom."

She nodded, unable to speak. Arms around his neck, she nuzzled his shoulder and kissed his lips. Such a perfect face he had. Her hand roamed his face, stroked his cheek, his ear, the curve of his throat.

So gentle she almost cried, he set her on the bed and undressed her while she lay gazing up at him. When she tried to sit, to reach him, to strip him, he shook his head, his mouth curled into a bawdy grin. "Let me feast on you?"

Again she nodded, still at a loss for words. But the gasps, the moans, and the sighs spilled from her. Cope's hands sparked life and electricity through her.

The room was too bright, so Dani found her voice. "The lights … turn them off?"

When he removed his hands and rose to switch off the lights, his absence filled her with an ache stronger than anything she'd ever experienced. Need overwhelmed her—need for his touch, his voice, his whole being.

"Oh, God, Robert. Please." But she couldn't have said what she begged him to do. It didn't matter—whatever he wanted was okay with her.

Cope lay next to her, mouth tasting her lips, hands exploring her, exciting her, sating the hunger within her that only he could satisfy. When his naked body covered hers, she came back with a shock, unable to remember him undressing.

Impatient to have him inside her, she slid a hand to his swollen penis, already covered with a condom, and guided him into her. Gratified at the strangled cry wrenched from him as he entered her, she wrapped her legs around him, wanting him deeper, deeper.

"Dani, Jesus. Oh, God. I'll pass out."

Tighter. She gripped him tighter, with her arms, her legs, and the muscles inside her. This was about uniting, not just physical release. But the release was there, and hers came first. Gasps, twitches, moans, and screams she muffled with closed lips heralded her climax and then triggered his.

Sweat trickled down his forehead, and she wiped it away with tender fingers. He collapsed onto her chest and rolled to his back, settling next to her. She snuggled against him, into the crook of his arm, her head on his chest. She peppered his chest with kisses and smiled in response to his grin.

"I can't get enough of you," he said and smoothed the sweat-damp hair from her face.

"Me too. You." She giggled, a surge of happiness making everything delightful. "Stay here tonight?" He hadn't done that before, and she wondered if asking him now would make him feel smothered. But the prospect of letting him walk out the door, leaving her alone, frightened her more than asking him to stay did.

"Of course."

Relaxed, happy, drowsiness overpowered Dani, and her lids drooped. When the apartment buzzer sounded, she jumped.

CHAPTER 18

Cope turned to Dani. "You expecting someone?"

"No, of course not. I'll be right back." She grabbed a robe from the hook on the back of the bedroom door and hurried to the foyer. She pressed the intercom button. "Hello?"

A belch and sniffling greeted her.

"Hello?"

"Dan—Dan—ni—" Henderson's voice hiccupped over the intercom.

"Greg?" She startled when Cope's hand dropped to her shoulder and his arm wrapped around her.

"Everything okay?" Cope's voice was mild, conversational, but she sensed the tension under it.

"Can I—" Braaack. "Can I come up?"

"Not a good time. Go home. You're drunk, and we've got an early shoot tomorrow." *The love scene tomorrow.*

"I just want to talk, babe."

Pressed against Dani's body, Cope went rigid.

"I'm not letting you up. Go home."

"You alone? I'll come up there and fuck your brains out. Hey? How about it? For old time's sake."

Cope released her, and she threw him a pleading look. He scowled and went to the bedroom. Terrified Henderson was driving Cope away, making him want to leave her, tears threatened, and her voice trembled when she spoke. "Go sleep it off, Greg."

Finger snapping away from the intercom, she choked off the sounds from the lobby entrance. Buzzes from the speaker followed her into the bedroom where Cope sat on the side of the bed, head in hands.

He met her gaze when she stepped into the room. "I walked away so I wouldn't be tempted to push you aside and say something regrettable.

Option two was to run down there and clean his clock, but I'm naked."

Dani sat next to him on the bed. "I thought you'd gone to get dressed and go home." She hadn't intended to admit that, but fear pushed it out.

"My beauty, I wouldn't do that to you."

The persistent buzzing penetrated awareness, and both turned to peer out the open bedroom door.

"Call security, Dani. They should have noticed by now he's a nuisance."

She checked the time. "It's not even nine o'clock, and he's drunk. Should I let him up?"

Cope's face darkened. "Why?"

"What if he does something stupid?"

"He's already done something stupid—he came here and bothered us. Call security and tell them to get him into a cab. Give them his home address, and they'll escort him out of here. If you let him come up, you're just reinforcing his manipulative behavior, and trust me, he wouldn't be happy to see me."

"But he'll be upset and mad at me."

Cope took her in his arms. "You're not responsible for his feelings or his reaction to you setting boundaries. Okay?"

Relieved, giving herself permission to refuse to let Henderson guilt her into doing what he wanted, she kissed Cope on the cheek. "You're right. I'll get him out of here, and we can carry on with our nice, quiet evening."

She called security and explained the situation to the guard on duty, who assured her he'd remove Henderson from the premises. She returned to the bedroom, heart skipping a beat when she saw Cope dressed.

At the sight of her expression, he strode to her and hugged her tight. "I'm not going anywhere. Don't look so scared. I'm not tired, and I thought we could watch TV."

"Mind if I stay in my robe?"

Instantly, his mouth pressed to hers. When he lifted his head again, he said, in a low growl, "If you stay in that robe, we might not end up watching TV."

"I'll risk it," she gasped.

His laugh filled her with that happiness she'd experienced earlier, and, taking his hand, she led him to the den. "I'll put the kettle on and make popcorn."

"Let me help." He followed her to the kitchen, and they fell into an easy routine.

She kept staring at him, drinking him in. His presence fed her, energized her, even as it comforted and offered peace she'd never had.

Later, after the movie, they settled back into bed and made love again. Snuggled in the shelter of Cope's arm, Dani wondered that she'd never desired this companionate silence before. None of the other men she'd slept with had wanted to just be with her. They'd always taken her out, showing her off like a trophy, or they'd fucked her without affection.

The next day's shooting schedule intruded then, and Dani's gut clenched with worry. Henderson had been drinking early in the evening and had shown up at her door. Even if security ensured he left here in a cab, there was no telling if he arrived home.

Knowing him as well as she did, she suspected he'd have directed the driver to take him to a club. Best-case scenario tomorrow would be if Henderson was too hung over to do the scene. Worst case? She could imagine some awful ones, and gnawing at them kept her up half the night despite Cope's reassuring presence. The closer daybreak came, the tenser she became.

When Dani finally drifted into an uneasy sleep, it was close to 3:00 AM, but that night, at least, there were no nightmares.

CHAPTER 19

Dani lay on the bed, a sheet draped over her chest and belly and tangled around her thighs. Since the scene involved shots of her breasts as specified in her contract, she didn't wear nude-toned pasties on her nipples. A flesh-colored pad covered her crotch.

Greg Henderson lay in bed beside her, wearing a cock sock over his penis, and he was stinking drunk. So far, Jake Ferguson had pumped him full of water, shot two takes, and given him one bathroom break. Dani had been grateful when Henderson returned from the bathroom smelling like mint and not vomit, and he appeared to have sobered up enough not to puke on her.

"You're so hot, babe."

"Fuck off, Greg." Dani kept her voice low, though the mics were probably picking up every word. The set was closed, which meant minimal crew and no other cast members present, but those who were stood nearby.

"You turn me on. I can't stop thinking about last time. Let's make this next take real. Come on. It'll win you another Oscar." He pressed up against her, his stiff, naked cock rubbing against her butt cheeks, and, shocked, she jerked away.

"I swear to God I'll have you fired if you don't fuck off right now. Put the sock back on." Annoyed that her voice trembled, Dani inhaled, held her breath, and then slowly exhaled.

"I know you want me, babe." Henderson snugged up against her. "He was in your apartment last night, wasn't he? Driver boy—your new boyfriend. Copeland isn't the man I am. Let me show you what a real man can do since you've obviously forgotten."

"Ready on the set." Ferguson's voice cut into the conversation, and Dani tried to settle her emotions to get the scene over with.

"Okay, lights."

The slate showing the scene and take clapped, and Ferguson counted down to action. Henderson's lips covered hers, and Dani responded, hands caressing his hair, the sheet sliding from her breasts.

His fingers pressed and squeezed her breasts. A knee slid between her legs, shoved them open. The sheet fell away, and Dani glimpsed the overhead camera getting the shot of Henderson's ass as it rose and fell on top of her.

Suddenly, his hand snaked between her legs and ripped away the pad. His cock poked between her legs, and she struggled, desperate to get out from under him. She opened her mouth to scream, and he pressed his mouth tight to hers, stifling the sound. He penetrated her. The tears flowed as Dani wrenched her mouth free, scratched his face, and then punched the side of his head.

"Get him off me. Help, please. Help me."

"Grab him," Ferguson shouted.

Oh, thank God, he's stopping it. The pressure on her body eased, and Henderson's penis slid from inside her.

Sobs wracked Dani's body, and shouts, cries, bangs, and struggles hurricaned around the bed. A woman from wardrobe wrapped a robe around Dani and hugged her. "You're okay, Miss Grayson. He's out of the room. Come with me." The wardrobe woman, Trina, escorted Dani to the dressing room.

Less than half-an-hour later, John Madden was at Dani's side. She'd ceased sobbing by then and refused to see anyone other than Trina or John. Trina had ordered tea, and by the time John burst into the room, Dani was nursing a cup of hot chai.

"What happened, honey?" John's gentle voice filtered through the haze insulating Dani.

She looked up and met his gaze.

"Greg." Too difficult to say more. She turned to Trina for help, and the wardrobe woman reached out a hand to rub Dani's back.

"Henderson raped Miss Grayson on camera, Mr. Madden."

Dani winced when she heard the words and lowered her gaze to the floor, unable to face John. How could she have not seen that coming? No one would believe her story. Her face flushed, and the sobs rose again, escaping her lips in hitching breaths.

John took the mug of tea from her shaking fingers and crouched to hug her. "It's okay, honey. I'm here, and I'll help you. Has anyone called the police?"

Loud sobs and a shake of Dani's head were the only response.

"Where is Henderson?"

"We don't know," Trina said, and Dani was grateful the woman was here to speak on her behalf.

"What does Jake say? What's he doing about it?"

"No one's come in here except me and you. Miss Grayson wanted to be alone. They let me phone you, but that's all. They told me not to call anyone else."

Cope. What will Cope say? Terrified at what her boyfriend might do if he found out, Dani considered keeping it quiet. If she pressed charges, the news would leak to the press, and the whole world would know. But if she kept it to herself, he'd be free to do it again, and she couldn't let that happen either.

Dani found her voice. "I want him fired."

"At the very least," John replied. "Can I leave you with Trina? I want to speak to Jake and contact Danger Play. I'm going to suggest they call the police. The longer they sit on it, the worse it'll look. They should act fast."

"No. Greg can't be arrested."

"Honey, he raped you." John's gaze flicked to Trina and then back to Dani. "Tell me what happened."

She pressed her palms to her face for a moment, then told John how she'd worried about the scene because Henderson had been drinking. Her biggest fear at the time was Henderson puking on her. "But then Greg tried to convince me to have sex with him. He had a hard-on and removed the sock. I should have made them stop the shoot right then."

That's what would burn her: she knew he'd been turned on, and she hadn't stopped the filming. A lawyer could exploit that. Henderson would be free to carry on as if nothing had happened while she'd have this degrading incident following her around.

Other actors might be afraid to do sex scenes with her, fearing she'd accuse them of rape. If the studios thought she was lawsuit happy or made false accusations, they wouldn't want her on their pictures. This could end her career.

"Call the lawyer, John. I need to understand my options before we call the police."

"Dani." He said nothing else, but if she inferred correctly, he wanted her to press charges.

"No." For emphasis, she shook her head. "Not until I understand the consequences. Greg was drunk, and he was out of his mind, wanting to get back together with me. We have a history. I was aware he was unstable, and I said nothing to Jake."

"Did you tell Greg no?"

And there it was: the start of the questions everyone would ask. What had the mics picked up, and who'd been listening? They must have captured the conversation but wouldn't have recorded anything until Dani and Henderson began simulating sex.

"Yes." Dani laughed, and it was bitter. "Greg argued with me even

82

though I'd told him to back off, and before I could say anything more, Ferguson called action. The scene started, and Greg raped me. He'll likely say he thought I was okay with it because I did the scene. I want him fired, but I doubt I can press charges."

"Of course you can."

A knock on the door interrupted, and Ferguson poked his head into the room. "Dani, angel, I'm so sorry. Tell me what happened."

"You were there, Jake. Henderson raped me." She tried to keep her voice even, but it had gone shrill when she'd spoken of the rape.

"Are you sure?"

"Are you doubting me? You think I'm lying? You've got to be fucking kidding. Or you think I'm confused?" Dani jumped up, knocking the chair over. "What else does it mean when someone sticks his dick in you even though you don't want him to? And he fucking stuck his dick in me even though I didn't want him to." She stifled a sob, but it was of rage now, not sorrow, fear, or anything else.

John stood in front of her, a protective, shielding move, and faced Ferguson. "You can't be serious. She's not making this up."

"Sorry, Dani. I'm not saying it didn't happen. I'm asking if maybe he got carried away in the moment and thought you were okay with it. You two have done this once before. I'll never forget what happened when you had on-camera sex during *Injury*."

Shame filled her then—at what she'd done before and at what had happened now, which would be colored by what she'd done before. After taking a deep breath, she looked Ferguson in the eyes, and said, "I want him fired. I won't work with him. Write him out of the script. Kill off his character. I haven't decided to press charges. That'll depend on what my lawyer advises, but either Greg goes, or I do."

Ferguson grimaced. "I'll talk to Danger Play. They hold the contracts. I've already left messages for them. I'm sure they'll call soon."

"Get it done, Jake," John said. "My client won't work under these conditions any longer. And she's done for today and tomorrow. When this gets sorted out, she'll return to work, but not before we're guaranteed that Greg Henderson is gone."

Ferguson promised to deal with it and left the room.

John dismissed Trina, helped Dani right the chair she'd knocked over, and put an arm around her. "Let's go home. Get dressed, honey. I'll drive you."

"Okay. Please don't leave the room—I can't face being alone right now. Just turn your back."

He obliged, and she dressed quickly, but with fumbling fingers. She couldn't seem to stop shaking. What if the studio made her continue working with Henderson? She couldn't do it. What if this ruined her career as much as if she pressed charges? If Henderson were on a picture, she might not be hired. If she couldn't work with him again, and he continued to get parts in large, commercial films, she'd be winnowed out of the business.

Tears threatened again, and she choked them down. *Stop it. You don't know that's how it'll go.*

But if history were any judge, it could. How many women had had their careers stagnate because they'd refused to sleep with someone who had power, authority, or influence?

Dani grabbed her purse, took a deep breath, and put an arm around John. "Please take me home. I can't stand it here another minute."

CHAPTER 20

The overarching sensation pervading her body, which was more an absence of feeling if she thought about it, was a floating numbness. Dani lay curled in the fetal position on the couch, a thick blanket covering her. John sat on the armchair ninety degrees and two feet from her head. The TV ran, mute. News headlines scrolled across the bottom, and the handsome newscaster flapping his gums filled the rest of the screen.

"You don't have to stay." Dani turned her head so John was in her field of vision.

Light faded from the room while afternoon melted toward evening. They'd been in Dani's apartment for hours though she wasn't sure how many. John had served tea. The large pot, the milk and sugar, and their mugs still sat on the coffee table. The tea service sat on a tray, the mugs on coasters. That was important. The coffee table was new, and it had been considerate of him to use the tray and coasters.

The recognition that her mind rambled moistened Dani's eyes. She ducked her face down so he wouldn't see. Every time the waterworks started, he became overly solicitous and concerned. Didn't he realize she just needed to cry?

"I'm not leaving you alone. Can we call Cope now?"

John had been pestering her to call Cope. Her boyfriend. The one who'd told her to watch out for Henderson, who'd asked her to let him know if Henderson ever did anything inappropriate. She'd promised, but how could she tell Cope what had happened? What if he blamed it on her?

"Dani? Honey, you need someone here. I don't want to leave you alone."

John wants to go home to his wife, his kids. Naturally, he wanted that—needed it—after what had happened today. No doubt, he wanted to let the domesticity and normalcy ease the stress. He could escape, and she wanted

85

him to. The fewer people to suffer over this the better.

She pictured Cope walking into the apartment, hurrying to comfort her, then finding out the sordid details. She'd talked to the lawyer, and he'd told her the case would be difficult to prosecute.

The footage from *Injury* proved she'd willingly done this with Henderson before, but Danger Play still planned to fire him. It boiled down to PR. Her eyes welled up. Some version of the story would go public regardless of what she wanted.

She sat up.

"Okay, I'll call Cope." She picked up her purse from the floor next to the couch and snatched the phone from it. The wheels were in motion. As soon as word leaked out that Henderson was off the picture, the media would dig. If they found out Dani was responsible and the reason for it, it'd be all over the news. That's not how she wanted Cope to hear of it. She punched the number to speed dial him.

"Robert Copeland speaking."

Thank God "Robert, it's me." Dani hiccupped, and her voice sounded thick with crying.

"What's wrong? Did something happen on the film? Is it Henderson?"

The accuracy of his suspicions offset the relief at hearing his voice. "Yes. Can you come over? I need you."

"What did he do?"

The fury in his voice frightened her. "I'll tell you when you get here. It's okay now, but I need you here. Can you get away?"

"Of course. I'll be right there."

The call ended, Dani told John one more time he could leave. Still, he insisted on staying until Cope arrived, though she could sense John's relief that Cope was on his way. Soon, John would hand her off, and he'd be free to enjoy the peace and quiet of his normal family.

Ashamed there was a time when she'd have tried to break that normal family up, Dani again pressed him to go. "Your wife will want you home. It's all right. I'm fine."

He stood, leaned down, kissed her cheek, and stroked her hair. "Okay, sweetie. But remember, I'm just a phone call away. Go to your appointment with Doctor Hadley tomorrow. Therapy does wonders even when you believe things are fine. Right now, they're not."

"I promised I'd go."

He left, and ten minutes later, Cope arrived. Dani ran to the door and threw it open, then realized she'd forgotten to check the peephole first. Guilt flashed across her face, but he either didn't see it or ignored it. He swept her into his arms and covered her in kisses. For perhaps the tenth time that day, she burst into sobs.

"What happened?" He lifted her in his arms and carried her to the

86

couch, letting the door slam shut behind him.

She raised her face to look into his eyes, so dark and hypnotizing. Her glance moved down his body, and she nuzzled her head into his neck.

One of his arms cradled her on his lap, and the other stroked her cheek. "What happened, Daniella? Tell me."

So she did, halting when the shame and embarrassment and fear overwhelmed her, but she did it dry eyed. The arm around her tightened its grip, the stroking on her face paused. His heart thudded against her chest when she wrapped her arms around him and clung to him.

"Did anyone call the police?" It was the first thing he said after listening to the story without interruption.

"No," she said in a whisper, eyes averted, because now he'd want to know why. So many valid reasons, but telling him would bring out more shame, and she'd have to admit their on-camera episode during *Injury*.

The dreaded word came out tinged with agony. "Why?"

"I can't. The lawyer thinks we'd lose, and I'd be dragged through the mud publicly. He advised me not to press charges."

"What does John say about that?"

Dani shifted to look into Cope's eyes. "He's not happy about it, but he's not pushing me to do it. The studio fired Greg." Saying his name left a foul taste in her mouth, and she grimaced. "They'll rewrite the script, use what footage they've got, and shoot other scenes to fill in the blanks. Ferguson might need to do a scene or two with Greg, and they still intend to pay him, but my scenes with him are done. Essentially, he's off the picture. His character will die, and I'll get a new partner."

Cope leaned back against the sofa, pulling her with him, his hand once again stroking her hair. "I knew that son-of-a-bitch still had a thing for you. I saw that interview he did after your mother's arrest. Was he drunk when he did this?"

"Not drunk, but not sober."

"Not sober means drunk, Dani."

"Not with Greg. I've seen him worse. He could still function."

"Clearly."

That made her laugh a little, and she actually felt lighter. "I'll see my therapist tomorrow?"

"Is that a question?"

"No." She smiled into his chest, so strong and reassuring. "I'm going. John insisted on making the appointment, and it might help."

"If you're asking my opinion, you should go. This must have traumatized you. I'm sorry it happened. What can I do to help?"

"You don't think it's my fault?" She said it in a small voice, timid, fearful. It had haunted her through the bulk of the afternoon while she'd quivered on the couch.

"You have a low opinion of me if you believe I'd blame you for being raped by a drunken jackass. Don't beat yourself up for what happened. It's not your fault. Henderson attacked you. He ignored you when you told him no. That's the definition of rape."

Relieved that Cope still wanted her, she sat up, spun around to straddle him, and kissed his lips. "Thank you for being so wonderful. Can we still go somewhere together on the weekend? I'm not working tomorrow, then there's a shoot on Saturday during the day, but I'm all yours by dinner time."

"I'll plan something special." He looked over her shoulder and frowned.

Wondering what had caught his eye, Dani turned around and gazed at the TV. An image of Henderson and Dani displayed behind the newscaster. She grabbed the remote and turned up the sound. "… made no comment. We will continue to update as the story unfolds."

"Oh, God. The media has the story already." Dani's heart froze. What had they found out? What had they told the world? And what was Greg Henderson saying about it?

CHAPTER 21

According to the media, Henderson was off the picture due to creative differences. The phone calls from reporters, which had died off while her mother's case languished waiting for the trial to start, sparked up again.

Dani had flashbacks to the morning she'd found out her father was dead when she awoke the next day to the phone ringing off the hook. Fooled once before, she didn't pick up this time and listened to the pleas for a statement over voice-mail.

The limo waited for her in the parking garage where the reporters couldn't get to her. The visit to the therapist went well, and Dani was happy she'd kept the appointment. When she returned to the apartment, the crush of reporters surrounding the building made her want to escape. Speed-dialing Cope, she asked him to meet her for lunch.

As the driver steered the car to a nearby restaurant, her nerves fluttered. This was their first time in public as a couple. At least they were meeting at a restaurant Cope favored. The paparazzi and her fans wouldn't expect her to show up there. Now, she wished she'd gone home and changed into something casual that wouldn't attract attention.

The car pulled up in front of the restaurant, and Mark came around to open her door. Dani stepped out, mindful of her short skirt and three-inch heels. Heat shimmered off the sidewalk, but she'd brought her suit jacket to cover the spaghetti straps of her tank top. Loose hair grazed her shoulders, falling in a cascade of ringlets. Everyone on the sidewalk turned to stare.

She gave a half-smile to a young boy about thirteen. When his gaze met hers, he turned to his mother and shouted, "Mom, that's Daniella Grayson. She *smiled* at me."

The mother turned doe eyes on Dani and stopped walking. "Miss Grayson, my son is such a huge fan of yours. I know you're probably busy, but could we get an autograph?"

Dani stopped and beamed a smile at the woman. She always had time for her fans, especially the polite ones. If it weren't for them, she wouldn't be where she was.

"Of course." She'd always felt too self-conscious to carry around photos of herself, but she had a pen and notepad.

She signed the paper for the boy, who said his name was Andrew, and handed it to him. Gaze falling to the mother's cell phone, she said, "Andrew, would you like your mom to take our picture with her phone?"

The boy looked as if he might pass out and nodded his head so vigorously she was afraid it would drop off. "Oh, man, yes, please. The guys won't believe this."

Dani let the mom snap a couple of pictures, but by then, a crowd had gathered, and others wanted photos and autographs. Not sorry she'd stopped for the young fan, but uneasy with the crowd building around her, Dani glanced at the door to the restaurant.

A polite smile on her face, she edged toward the entrance. "Thank you, everyone, I need to get inside now, or I'll be late for my date."

A mic appeared under her chin, and a woman wearing a press badge blocked her path. "Adriana Miller, Miss Grayson. TETN. Who's waiting for you inside? Is it Greg Henderson? Are you back together?"

Dani shook her head and pulled away, scanning the area for Mark or Cope. The restaurant was casual and didn't have security at the door. The crowd pressed in around her, and the reporter continued to shove the microphone in her face.

"Miss Grayson, what creative differences caused Greg Henderson to leave *Injury 2?*"

"I'm sorry, but I can't discuss that."

A man gripped her arm and pulled her to him. "I'll help you, Miss Grayson."

Dani shook with fear when he put an arm around her. Purse hugged to her chest, she tried to extricate herself from the man's embrace. He inched her through the crowd but headed away from the restaurant.

"No, please. I need to get into the restaurant." She'd been so stupid to come here, to think they could have a quiet lunch. A sob escaped her lips, of frustration, of anger, of dread. Cope wouldn't know where she was. Panic rose, and she twisted away from the man who had his arm around her.

"Dani?" Cope's voice penetrated the roar of the crowd.

Oh, thank God. "Robert!" She saw his head above the sea of people around her and waved at him.

"Miss Grayson, is that man, Robert, your boyfriend?" The reporter was back.

A desire to shove the mic into the woman's face became almost overwhelming, but Dani restrained herself. Gaze locked on Cope's, she waved her hand to make sure he didn't lose her in the crowd. At least they were both tall.

After what seemed an eternity, the crowd in front of her parted, though not willingly. Cope elbowed his way through to her, and she fell into his arms. Hands on each side of her face, he tilted her head up and planted a kiss on her lips.

"Come on. I'll get us in there."

That he did it without the involvement of a security team or the police force impressed Dani. No fans were harmed or offended. Once inside, she relaxed, though she continued to huddle under Cope's strong, capable arm.

He guided her to the table where he'd been sitting when the crowd outside had caught his attention. "This is why you need a bodyguard and not just a chauffeur."

"Okay." She wasn't going to argue, remembering the guy who'd put his arm around her and tried to steer her away. "I'm sorry. This young kid wanted my autograph, and it snowballed. I didn't think I'd make it in here. Thank God, you came out."

"It's not your fault, but I don't want you going out without a bodyguard again. I've got connections. There's a guy who'll be working for me once I open for business who can drive you around starting tomorrow. I can take care of the details, but you'll have to authorize the tab."

"Okay. I trust you." *Trust you.* Yes, she trusted Cope with her life. The urge to jump across the table and cover him in kisses hit her and made her smile.

"What's with the evil grin?"

"Just thinking how much I want to, well, attack you where you sit. One drawback of going to a restaurant to eat is you can't fornicate in public. Maybe we should just stay home for meals."

He chuckled, and they both looked up when the waitress appeared. The rest of the lunch date turned out to be a pleasant and relaxing interlude. At the end of it, Dani waited in the restaurant while Cope had the limo brought around, and then walked with him to where Mark stood waiting. Despite the crush of reporters and flashing cameras, she gave Cope a passionate farewell kiss and promised him a nice dinner when he came over that night.

CHAPTER 22

The Saturday shoot rescheduled to the Monday shoot as the search for a new partner for Dani got underway, and the script was rewritten. Cope took an early day on Saturday since Dani didn't have to go to the studio. He arranged to pick her up in the late afternoon and told her to wear casual clothes—shorts and a T-shirt and flip-flops or sneakers.

Unable to contain her excitement, she took longer to dress for this casual date than she'd taken for the fanciest date she'd ever had. She settled on denim capris, a white, midriff-baring tank top, and canvas sneakers.

Neutral makeup and a tousled hairstyle enhanced her almond eyes and highlighted her cheekbones. When she verified the effect in the mirror, the results pleased her. She was doubly pleased when Cope expressed appreciation of her efforts with kisses and touches.

Forty minutes into the drive, the route became disturbingly familiar.

"Are we headed to your parents' place?" Dani tried to keep the anxiety out of her voice and thought she'd succeeded.

"Okay, ya got me. That's where we're going, but not to visit them. I knew I wouldn't be able to keep it to myself for too long. The beach on my parents' property is a great place for a picnic. I figured that still counts as 'going out,' but we won't get swamped by paparazzi or fans."

Eyes wide, Dani clapped her hands and bounced in her seat like a kid.

He turned to watch her and smiled. "You're so cute."

She laughed, loud and delighted. "I can't recall when I've been this excited to go on a date. What a wonderful idea."

The car pulled off the highway, and Cope followed the route to the cliffs. Dani now considered that beach the location of their first unofficial date. She shuddered at the memory of how that had ended. One day, she supposed, she'd look back on it and laugh, but that day hadn't arrived.

Twenty minutes later, the car sat parked at the head of the trail, their cell phones turned to silent and tucked away. They sat on a large blanket on the sand amidst a spread of crusty breads; tapenade; a variety of cheeses; a container with a mixture of greens, sliced fresh tomatoes sprinkled with basil; pickles; chopped vegetables; and fruit.

"You're amazing." She beamed at him, picked up a glass of sparkling peach juice, and sipped, appreciating the change from plain mineral water.

"You inspire me. I love that radiant smile on your face, and I'll do anything to make it appear. It's fun to think of things that'll make you forget everything but us."

Touched, she raised the glass in *salud*, and Cope picked up his own goblet and clinked it to hers. "To us."

They ate, enjoying the sunshine, the food, and each other. The ocean lent a romantic ambience.

After the meal, Cope packed up the basket, removed his and Dani's shoes, and pulled her up for a walk in the surf.

"So cliché, isn't it?" he said. "A walk along the beach. We'll milk it and stay until sunset. Today, we won't be interrupted. Cell phones are off and no one can comment on it."

"John doesn't worry anymore when I'm with you."

"Does he know you're with me now?"

A wave crashed against her legs, splashing her thighs, and she backed out to shallower water, laughing. She pulled Cope after her and put her arm around his waist.

"Yes. I tell him when I go out if I'm not taking the limo and the bodyguard. I could resent it, but it's because he cares, and I can't fault him for that."

He nodded. "I can't be with you twenty-four-seven, so I feel better knowing he's watching out for you too."

On tiptoe, Dani turned to Cope, clasped her hands behind his neck, and kissed him, a deep, sensuous, soul-baring kiss. "Let's go back to the blanket."

He reached up a hand and fisted it in her hair. "What do you have in mind?" His voice verged on a growl.

Before she could answer, his arms encircled her, and his mouth covered hers, devouring.

Across the ocean, the sun hovered near the horizon. The scent of fish, moss, and salt spray wafted up with every breeze. Her hair floated around their heads like seaweed.

He disconnected, put a finger under her chin, and kissed her nose.

"I brought dessert and tea. If it gets chilly, there's an extra blanket to snuggle under." He wiggled his brows and licked his lips. "It'll be cozy and private."

Energized by love for him, Dani threw her arms around him and kissed his cheek. "I'll race you back."

She released him and tore off along the shore, kicking up clods of sand and splashes of water as she flew toward their nest.

His shout followed her. "No fair—you had a head start." He chased after her.

When she reached the blanket, she fell onto it, then rolled on her back and waited for him to catch up.

He dropped beside her, then rolled on top of her, kissing her and stroking her as if he couldn't get enough physical contact.

"Wait." She pulled away, laughing, and grabbed her bag. She took out her cell phone and switched to camera mode. "Selfie! Lean in, Cope."

He laughed and pressed his face against hers, the tiny stubbles on his cheek and chin tickling her skin. The phone wobbled as she adjusted the position, and then she took three photos.

"This one's perfect." She showed him the picture. "I'll send it to you."

She switched off the phone, stuck it back in her purse, and turned her attention back to her beautiful guy. Afraid she'd say the "L" word if she didn't do something fast, she pulled his head down and kissed him. The urge to say she loved him became overwhelming, but she feared it was too soon. What if he didn't feel the same way?

"Cope?" She hadn't intended to speak. That had just popped out. "I love today. Thanks for doing all this." There. That wasn't a lie, but missed the mark from what she wanted to say.

She couldn't stop smiling and thought she'd look back on this afternoon as one of the most perfect in her life. Yes, she'd experienced more trauma recently, but Cope's romantic gesture had erased all worries for a few hours and made her feel loved. She really did love this day.

***

Monday morning, the filming got underway just after sunrise. The cast and crew tiptoed around Dani, more polite and solicitous than usual, which made it difficult for her to focus.

Kind of them to consider her feelings, but it was hard enough to continue with the film without others' behavior highlighting that everything was uncomfortable.

"I saw your new boyfriend in the tabloids, Miss Grayson," Trina said. At least the wardrobe woman still acted normal around her, still chatted away as if life could continue no matter what had happened.

Dani wanted to smile, but forced herself to hold still while Sandra, a makeup artist, worked on her face.

Trina fiddled with Dani's outfit, a designer suit which adorned a dressmaker's dummy, preparing it for the next scene. "He's hot. *The*

Tattletale had a whole article on how Robert Copeland rescued you at that restaurant on Friday."

Forcing her eyebrows to stay still, Dani attempted to speak with minimal lip movement. "That was fast."

It came out as "at uz as," but Trina apparently could translate, because she replied with "Yeah, pictures and everything. They must have rushed it through."

Unable to help it, Dani smiled, with the unfortunate timing of doing it just as Sandra touched the lip liner to Dani's upper lip.

"Oops. Well, we'll fix that." Sandra set the lip pencil on the table and snatched up a cotton pad with makeup remover on it.

"Sorry. I wasn't thinking."

"No harm. I'll just clean it off, and we'll start again."

Dani stayed silent this time, lips slightly parted, and Sandra continued her work.

Happy to have a captive audience, Trina continued to chat. "Those clips of you two coming out of the restaurant looked gorgeous, and what a kiss. Saw that on the entertainment news. I guess Mr. Copeland knows what it's like to be followed around by the paparazzi now. I hear women are chasing him. You'd think they'd understand he's taken."

The words, innocent enough, caused a sinking sensation in Dani's stomach. Women were stalking Cope, pestering him, and maybe throwing themselves at him. She realized she was speculating, but Trina was right— Cope was hot. A feeling of being unworthy seeped into Dani.

Stop it. Cope wants to be with you and no one else.

Yes, but for how long—especially if reporters and groupies made it difficult for him to go about his daily routine? Even after two years of it, Dani still wasn't used to having her every move monitored by the public, but it went with the career she'd chosen.

She'd understood from the start that if she succeeded in film, her life would be under a klieg light. But Cope was a businessman, not an entertainer. He might not tolerate the intrusion, and sooner or later, he might decide he'd had enough.

***

Patrick Mullaly, Felicity Sanderson's new partner, stroked Dani's cheek. "We all miss Charles. We must learn to carry on without him. He'd want you to be happy, Felicity. Whatever you need, I'm here for you."

She clasped the hand and held it for a moment, then released it. She turned on her heel and moved away from Patrick, a tall, lanky man whose real name was Mike Erwin. Dani hung her head, allowing a tear to drip down her cheek.

"How will I live without him? Charles was my life."

"You're grief-stricken, and that's understandable, but you're getting careless. Charles would have my head if he saw you do the shit you've been doing. You're risking your neck because you're so hell-bent on catching the bastard who killed him. But if you don't take care, that maniac will catch you first."

"I'm not being careless, Mike. Pat. Oh, shit, sorry."

"Cut." Ferguson waved his hand, and the cameras stopped rolling.

"I'm sorry, Pat." Dani smiled at Mike, who mock punched her shoulder.

"It's okay, shweetheart."

She laughed. "Is that supposed to be Bogie?"

"What if it is?" He raised an eyebrow. "You're not old enough to remember Bogie."

"Neither are you. You're only twelve years older than I am. I know my film history, and I've watched his movies. *Casablanca.* Love it."

"Okay, you two. I'm thrilled you're getting along, but can we get this rolling? We've already lost over two days." Ferguson paused, shot Dani an apologetic glance, and asked them to start from the top.

It took a dozen takes to get the scene right, and Dani relaxed as the day continued. Mike was a pleasure to work with, and she realized that, in the past, she'd have fallen hard for him. He was married, though, and gave her the impression he was faithful to his wife of five years, who was pregnant with their first child.

On their lunch break, Dani asked him about it. The two sat in his dressing room, Dani sipping on a mug of broth and picking at a salad, Mike eating a burger and fries.

"How has your fame affected your marriage? Is it hard on your wife?"

"Not terribly. She sometimes gets followed around by reporters if I'm doing a picture that's made the news. This one will give her more of that than any of the others I've done. So far, she's taken it in stride."

"It might be more of a problem when the baby's born, don't you think?" Dani shuddered at the thought of reporters following her around if she had a new baby. She'd be so worried about the crush of people, the mics, and the constant invasion of privacy.

"I guess. We'll hire a bodyguard if it gets worse."

"Talk to my boyfriend, Cope. He's starting up a limo service that will offer drivers who double as bodyguards."

Mike dragged a French fry through a puddle of ketchup and stuck it in his mouth. "Leave me his contact info and I'll call him. I saw the footage of you getting mobbed at the restaurant. You could've used a bodyguard yourself then."

She finished chewing a bite of lettuce. "You sound like Cope. He's got someone for me. The guy seems nice though he doesn't laugh much. What will your wife say about a bodyguard following her around?"

"If it protects our baby, she'll be on board with it."

Dani considered. "I guess when you have a baby, you'll do anything to protect it." As the implications of what she'd just said sank in, Dani's mouth twisted. That had never been the case with her own mother.

A longing for a normal, caring mother swept over her. What would it be like to experience unconditional love? The possibility existed that with Cope, she'd discovered the answer, if she could just manage not to ruin it.

CHAPTER 23

After filming wrapped for the day, Dani arrived home, showered off the heavy makeup and her character, and threw on a pair of jeans and a T-shirt. Feet bare and hair tied back in a ponytail, she padded out to the kitchen to start dinner. While she set the ingredients for a veggie stir fry on the counter, she let her mind wander back to the publicity Cope was getting from their relationship.

Perhaps it wasn't so bad and worked in his favor, giving the limo business a boost. On the heels of that thought came the worry he'd have multitudes of gorgeous women seeking his services.

She sighed. Infidelity had been a feature in her parents' relationship. Even at five, she'd sensed the unusual way her mother had behaved around other men, and the way other women had been around her father. Dani didn't think her dad had messed around. She frowned. Maybe she was making him out to be a better person than he was because he was dead and her mother had been so awful.

She picked up a zucchini and the chopping knife when a buzzing caught her attention. Dropping everything onto the cutting board, she went to grab the cell phone from her purse.

A glance at the call display showed Greg Henderson. She scowled and let it go to voice-mail. When the beep sounded, she called the service to retrieve the message.

"Dani, I'm sorry. Please, let me return to the film. Call me, babe. Let's talk about it."

She stared at the phone, unsure what to do and tempted to delete the message and forget about it. Finger poised to do just that, she stopped. If she ignored him, would he show up at her apartment again? Not wanting to take that chance, she punched in Henderson's number.

"Baby, I'm s' glad ya called." Slurred.

"What do you want, Greg?"

Heavy breathing flowed out of the receiver. She wrinkled her nose in distaste and glanced at the clock—not even six yet and he was already drunk.

"Leave me alone. Get help for your drinking problem."

"I don't need help drinking. It's not a problem." A bray of laughter. "I need help with my Dani problem. I've got a hard-on for you, babe, and it's making me ache. You're giving me blue balls. Wanna see? I can be there in a minute."

"Sleep it off and go join AA or see a therapist. I don't want you back on the set, and this behavior validates my decision. Damn it, Greg, you raped me."

"No, babe, you're wrong. I thought you wanted to fuck, you know, like before. It was a mistake."

"That's your story, then? You know damn well that's not what happened. Stay away from me and don't call again, or I'll press charges." She disconnected, hands shaking, and dropped to the couch, trying to compose herself. With her breath coming in shallow gasps, her whole body shook. A sob caught in her throat. One phone call. It took one phone call from that bastard, and she was unnerved beyond the ability to function.

A few minutes later, the doorbell chimed.

Cope. Thank God. Dani glanced at the clock. A few minutes early, too. Happy, she ran to the door, unlocked it, and threw it open, realizing as the door swung toward her she'd again opened it without checking the peephole.

"Ack, Cope, sorry I—"

It was as far as she got. Greg Henderson staggered inside, pushing the door closed behind him as he shoved Dani aside.

"How'd you get into the building? Get out. Now." Dani tried not to let her voice quiver and failed.

Henderson advanced on her, and she staggered back a few paces, almost reaching the coffee table in the living room. "I mean it, Greg. Get out of here."

"I just want to talk to you, babe. You hurt me. I need you. I've always loved you. We should be together. I'm sorry for everything. Let me fix it."

"There's nothing to fix. I don't want to be with you. We have no relationship anymore. You killed it. Your drinking, your abuse, and your womanizing destroyed what we had—which wasn't anything healthy to begin with."

For a drunk, he moved quickly, landing in front of her, oozing alcohol from every pore and wafting it out of his mouth into her upturned face. Rough hands gripped her upper arms, and she struggled to push him away, but he remained rooted.

"Kiss me. You'll see the spark's still there. You want me—I know you want me. That fucking boy you're seeing isn't man enough for you."

"You're repeating yourself, Greg. Get out now!" The last bit came out a scream of frustration. She twisted, struggled, but he held on tight, the pressure of his fingers on her arms squeezing until a sob of pain escaped her lips.

"Please. Let go. You're hurting me." For the first time, fear entered her voice. She glanced at the clock again. Cope wasn't due for another ten minutes. "Please." Whispered begging.

But he pulled her into the circle of his arms. His mouth covered hers, probing, hungry, and breath sour with whatever he'd been drinking. When he released one of her arms, she tried to push him away, but his iron chest remained pressed to her. Something tore and Dani realized it was her T-shirt.

"You little slut—not wearing a bra. For lover boy? You're mine, Dani. That fucking Copeland can settle for sloppy seconds." Henderson's large hand moved to her exposed breasts while his other hand continued to grip her arm.

As he forced her to the ground, his body crushing hers, Dani's fear escalated to terror. Tears streamed from her eyes. "Please. Stop. You're hurting me. No! I don't want to be raped again. Please."

"Rape? You fucking slut. You stupid bitch." He held her head motionless between his palms and spit in her face once and then again. One hand fumbled with the button of her jeans while she struggled, choking on sobs, the spittle smearing on her face.

"Tell me you want me, bitch. I know you want me. You'll scream for me now."

Her peripheral vision caught the swing of the door, and then Cope was there, ripping Henderson off her.

"Call nine-one-one, Dani, now." He dragged Henderson up by the back of the shirt, whirled him around, and punched him in the face.

She crawled to her purse and grabbed the cell phone. She made the call, forcing her fingers to press the right numbers and screaming at the dispatcher to hurry, please hurry. The woman's assurance that the police were on the way pushed through the numbness. Dani dragged herself to the intercom, ready to let the police into the building.

Henderson had hit the floor, but now struggled to get up, and blood from his nose dripped onto her carpet.

"Don't fucking move!" Cope screamed at him. "Sit there until the cops get here. You won't worm your way out of this one. She's got an honest-to-God witness now."

Outside, sirens screamed. *The police.* In a haze, Dani buzzed the cops into the building and then sat huddled on the floor while Cope ushered them into the unit. Henderson made another move to get up, and this time, the police dealt with him.

Cope rushed to Dani's side, hugged her, and covered the top of her head with kisses. "Okay, my beauty, we'll clean you up. Let's take a few pictures first. We'll need the evidence." The last came out in a venomous punch of air.

Dazed, Dani let Cope take the photos with his cell phone, her hands fluttering over her breasts in an attempt to hide her nakedness. An officer removed Henderson from the apartment while his partner asked Dani to relate what had happened. The cop's face was serious but kind, and he introduced himself as Officer Bradley.

Cope put an arm around Dani and helped her settle on the couch. "I'll get a wet cloth to wipe your face and a clean shirt. I'll be right back, darling."

She remained silent, arms still hugging her chest, but nodded to let him know she was okay enough to let him go. The cop stood and waited, back turned, while Cope helped her clean up and put on a shirt.

Curled up in the corner of the couch, she listened to Cope describe the scene he'd stumbled onto when he'd arrived at the apartment. The story made her cringe and brought tears to her eyes once more.

"She begged him to stop. He'd have raped her if I hadn't shown up right then," Cope concluded.

The officer turned to Dani. "Have you had any alcohol, Miss Grayson?"

"No." To emphasize the point, she shook her head. "I don't drink when I'm in the middle of a film shoot. It harms my performance."

"Okay. Tell me what happened."

So she told him, reliving the horror of Henderson, who she'd once loved and would've considered marrying, attacking her. How messed up on booze and drugs had she been to not recognize what a douche he was? At least she'd come to her senses and backed out of the relationship.

Afraid that Cope would get mad at her, she admitted opening the door without checking to see who was there. "I was expecting Cope—Robert." Dani threw a worried glance at Cope.

"It's okay, honey." He smiled encouragement and patted her hand.

Reassured, she continued the story until the point where Cope arrived and hauled Henderson away before he could rape her.

The interview over, Officer Bradley left Dani his card and told her to call him if she remembered anything she wanted to add to the statement. She thanked the officer, and when he left, she allowed herself to collapse into Cope's arms.

"Okay. It's okay. I'm here. No one will hurt you now." His voice soothed her, permitted her to release more tears.

"I'm so sorry. I should've used the peephole."

"You made a mistake. It's too late now to worry about what you should have done. Next time, check. Promise me? No matter how excited you are I've arrived, please check the peephole first?"

The weight of it eased a little at his kindness. "Yes, I promise."

He suggested she take a shower while he worked on dinner, and, relieved that everything would be all right, Dani left the room. The TV clicked as it powered on, and its soothing drone followed her down the hall and into her bedroom.

The scent of flowery shampoo filled her nostrils, and she scrubbed and lathered, the thought of Henderson's saliva in her hair compelling her to repeat the process three times. It turned out to be the longest shower she'd had in her life. By the time she was clean, dried, and dressed in a comfortable T-dress, the tension had left her.

Silence greeted Dani from the open bedroom door, and she figured Cope had turned off the TV. But she didn't hear the clatter of pots and pans or the sizzle of stir fry, and she didn't smell food cooking. Stomach queasy, she rushed out into the living room.

Cope sat on the armchair, face white, the muted television showing the current weather report. Chopped vegetables sat on the kitchen counter. The pot of water on the stove sat stone cold on the front left element, and the package of pasta lay on the counter unopened.

Anxiety knotting her stomach, Dani whispered, "Robert, what is it?"

CHAPTER 24

Cope stood and strode across the living room, stopping when he reached Dani. "Why didn't you tell me you own Star Power Investments?"

Stomach dropping, she gasped. "Where did you hear that?"

"The news. It's all over the news that my girlfriend is setting me up in business."

Frightened of his raised voice, she backed away from him. "Cope, I didn't think it should matter. I had minimal influence on the deal."

"But you were involved, and you knew I was dealing with them, yet you didn't say a word to me. Don't you have any respect for me?"

"Of course I do," she whispered.

He turned away from her. "Do you have a girlfriend you can call?"

Dani put a hand on his shoulder, fear making her nauseated. "Why? Where are you going?"

His shoulders shrugged, throwing her hand off, and he returned to the living room couch. "Call your girlfriend so you're not alone. I need time to think. I'll call my lawyer to see if I can back out of the contract."

"You can't." Voice still a whisper, her face flushed with shame.

"I can't?" His eyes narrowed, and his mouth twisted into a scowl. "Why not?"

"The process is in motion. Since Star Power transferred the funds to your account, you'd lose a lot of money if you tried to back out. Please, don't go. We'll discuss it."

"Call your friend, Dani. Now." He stood and paced between the coffee table and the door. "I don't want to leave you alone—not after what happened to you earlier. But I can't stay. So I'll wait for your friend to get here, and then I'm leaving. Do you understand?"

Numb, she picked up her cell phone and called Liz, who promised to be right over, no questions asked. Dani's throat threatened to close, and, knees shaking, she sank to the couch.

"Sit, Robert. Please? Don't just stand there."

"I'll wait here."

Breath hitching, she tried to hold back the tears until he was gone. Gone. She'd feared all along that what she had with Cope was too good to last. "Won't you let me explain?"

"Not now." His face softened as their gazes locked, and a spark of hope kindled inside her. But not for long.

"I love you, but I can't be with a woman who manipulates and lies to me. You went behind my back. You knew I didn't want help from anyone, even my parents, but that didn't matter to you."

"No, you don't understand. I love you, too."

He held up a hand, stopping her. "Not now. I can't bear your excuses right now. Respect me enough to give me that much."

The intercom buzzed. He pressed the button and asked who was there. Liz responded and he told her to come on up. When the doorbell rang, he pressed his eye to the peephole, exaggerating his moves. Any other time, Dani would have found that amusing. Now, it broke her heart.

He opened the door, and Liz stepped inside, immediately rushing to Dani's side. "Oh, honey, are you okay?"

Dani directed her gaze at the floor and nodded, but the tears overflowed her eyes and streamed down her cheeks.

"That bastard. I hope they lock him up forever."

Through choked sobs, Dani said, "I'm not crying because of Greg." She lifted her head to look at Cope—beg him to stay—and saw he wasn't there.

"Oh, God, Liz, what have I done? He's gone." She tumbled into Liz's arms and let the tears flow.

***

Liz stroked Dani's back while she choked out her story. "I let the team decide whether to lend him the money or not. If it wasn't a viable investment, they could've said 'no.' "

"Did you tell him that?"

"I tried. But he refused to let me talk. What am I going to do?" She didn't want to beg him, but she also didn't want to lose a relationship with potential.

"How'd he find out you own the investment company?"

"The news, which makes it so much worse. God knows what they said."

The two women exchanged glances.

"One way to find out," Liz said.

Dani grabbed the remote control from the coffee table, flicked to the news channel, and turned up the sound. A global news story played, and they waited for breaking news to scroll around again.

When it did, Greg Henderson's arrest was the lead story. Reporters following Henderson and hanging out in front of Dani's apartment building had caught him entering the complex and then later being led out by the police. The anchor, Lisa Knowles, an older woman in a navy business suit, face neutral, described the litany of charges: attempted rape, assault, resisting arrest, and assaulting a police officer. Henderson had apparently punched the police officer leading him away.

The video footage flicked to Dani and Cope kissing in front of the limo outside the restaurant at which they'd had their first lunch date.

Tears blurred Dani's vision, and she reached for a tissue.

Knowles mentioned Dani's relationship with Cope while a montage of images on the screen flashed behind the newscaster.

Cope at a restaurant; Dani coming out of a store; Cope and Dani exiting a restaurant; and Cope entering the building where his limo service headquartered. The camera closed in on the scene, the image freezing while Knowles described Cope's business and his backers at Star Power.

"Star Power, owned by Robert Copeland's girlfriend, Daniella Grayson, funds the venture." The camera panned out, and Knowles turned to her co-anchor, a middle-aged man with a cleft chin. "Must be nice to have friends in rich places, am I right, George?"

A chill went up Dani's spine, and she felt sick.

"Can you call someone a sugar baby if they're older than their benefactor, Lisa?" George laughed, and Knowles chuckled in response.

"You wouldn't think this guy needed to be a kept man since his parents are wealthy. I guess if Mom and Dad don't help you get your start, there's always a rich girlfriend."

Bile rose in Dani's throat, and she fought the urge to vomit. No wonder Cope was so angry with her. The media had twisted her intentions and made him look like a gold digger.

"Oh my God, Liz. Oh, God." Dani buried her head in her hands and sobbed.

Liz placed a hand on Dani's back and with gentle strokes tried to soothe her.

CHAPTER 25

In the days following Henderson's arrest, the publicity machine geared into overtime and Dani saw her face, Henderson's face, and Cope's face everywhere she looked. The headlines made her cringe and brought tears to her eyes. The media referred to Cope as "sugar baby" and "kept man," running with the terms flung out so carelessly by the newscasters on that first day.

Work on the film occupied Dani's days—and even her evenings when the shoot ran long. Her nights were lonely and cold, despite the heatwave that gripped the city. Cope didn't call, and Dani, though tempted to text or phone him, held back, giving him his space. She distracted herself by spending more time at the organization for abused children where she volunteered.

She kept tabs on Cope and the progress he made getting his limo service open for business through Star Power. The media noticed their separation and reported on it. A tabloid printed pictures of Cope at a restaurant with a sexy blonde woman. Katherine. Dani found the paper on a table in the lobby of her apartment building when she returned from work late one evening. She snagged it, read it, and then shredded it while the tears streamed down her face.

That moment was the closest she came to raiding her liquor cabinet. She went as far as opening the door and removing a bottle of tequila. A memory of Greg Henderson staggering into her apartment and ruining his career popped into her head, and she put the bottle back. Determined to avoid turning to alcohol, she locked the bar, forced herself off the floor, and stumbled to the kitchen to find something to eat.

A small salad would put healthy food in her body, and she thought her stomach could accept it without rebelling. Her appetite had been abysmal since Cope left. While she ate, sitting at the kitchen table, resisting the temptation to turn on the news, she wondered what she would do if he refused to see her again.

Their time together had been so blissful—at least, according to Dani. How could he be so angry with her he'd give that up? Maybe it hadn't been as blissful for him. If it was so easy for him to leave her, better it had happened before they'd made a serious commitment to one another.

How sad that the one time they'd said the 'L' word to each other it'd been when he'd walked out on her, perhaps forever. She dropped her fork onto the table when the tears dripped into her salad, covered up the barely-touched greens, and stuck it in the fridge.

She glanced at the clock, which read 9:06 PM. She went to her purse and grabbed her phone. If Liz was available, they could meet up and go to a club. It'd been ages since Dani had gone out.

Her girlfriend wasn't home, but Dani, craving people, decided she'd go to Vibrations alone. The club was one she'd frequented before she'd dated Cope, and she'd know enough of the regulars there to feel comfortable. If she stayed home, she'd mope and wallow in self-pity, and she'd had enough of that shit.

An hour later, Dani entered the club. Music throbbed around her and she made her way to the bar, waving to the people she knew. Soon, a group formed around her. After ordering a cranberry spritzer, Dani sat in a booth with a group of acquaintances she didn't realize she'd missed until she saw them again.

"How's the film coming along?" said Eric Wayan, the young man sitting on Dani's right. A scruffy beard offset his bright blue eyes and handsome face. Perhaps he was trying to give the illusion of fullness to a slim, tapered face. She didn't like the bearded look, but Eric's was neat and trim and gave him a bad-boy appearance that attracted her.

She smiled. "Great. We're shooting every day. I can't stay long tonight, but I had to get out."

"Care to dance?" He stood and offered her his hand.

Why not? She'd decided to have fun tonight despite that hollow space in her gut where Cope's love used to be.

"Okay." She tossed back the rest of her drink and followed Eric out onto the dance floor.

Somehow, she had fun. While she didn't get Cope out of her head, Eric at least made the evening a pleasant distraction. He kept her dancing and made her laugh. At midnight, she noticed the time and realized she'd killed the night. With an early-morning shoot, she'd better get home.

"I have to leave." Hoarse from screaming over the music all evening, Dani gestured at the doors to make sure Eric got the message.

"Okay. Would you like me to drive you?"

Dani shook her head. "I have my driver here."

"Can I see you again? Will you go out for dinner with me tomorrow?"

About to refuse, she considered that if she stayed in tomorrow, she'd spend the evening lost and heartbroken. Far better to get out and keep busy, though she wondered if that meant she was using Eric.

"Okay, but it's not a date."

Eric smiled. "Is there something wrong with dating me?"

"I'm getting over a breakup. I don't want to give you the wrong idea."

He took her hand and pressed it to his cheek. "It's okay. I know you and your boyfriend just split up. His loss. I don't want to replace him. No pressure. Just me taking you out for a nice dinner—no strings."

His hands were warm and soothing. She inhaled deeply and then exhaled slowly, trying to rid herself of the feeling that a date was admitting that what she'd had with Cope was over. The thought brought tears to her eyes again, and she bit her lip and held her breath, attempting to get control of her emotions.

"Yes. I'll go out for dinner with you tomorrow. Text me the details, and I'll meet you at the restaurant."

"Why don't you give me your address and phone number, and I'll come and get you? I'll drive."

She considered. John and Cope wanted her to take the limo wherever she went, and Ryan Pearlman, the bodyguard Cope had selected, followed her into whatever establishment she entered. She glanced over at the bar, where Ryan sat waiting for her, nursing a coffee.

But Henderson was in jail—no possible threat there, Cope didn't give a shit, and John, well, she'd worry about John's reaction if he ever found out. Fuck the bodyguard.

"Okay. Give me your cell phone."

Eric handed her his phone, and she input her information. He agreed to pick her up at eight o'clock, and Dani signaled to Ryan that she was ready to go.

Back in the car, Dani kicked off her sandals and massaged her sore feet while Ryan drove home. Tired, but feeling lighter than she had in days, Dani reclined in her seat and stared out the window.

Up ahead loomed Cope's building. She wondered what he was doing tonight and thanked her good sense she wasn't drunk. Even sober she wanted to pick up her phone and call him. If she'd been drinking, he'd have gotten a call similar to the one Henderson had given Dani—rambling, half-incoherent, and ingratiating.

As the car sailed past the skyscraper where he lived, Dani pressed her nose against the window and wished with all her heart that that was her destination.

CHAPTER 26

The date started out well enough. Eric picked Dani up in a sleek Corvette convertible. After riding around in limos for so long, she thrilled at the wind whipping her hair, and the sultry, humid evening charged with excitement. Eric's fair hair and tan complexion contrasted with Dani's dark locks and pale skin. When she had caught their reflection in the lobby doors, she'd felt a measure of smugness. If their pictures made it into tomorrow's papers, they'd look spectacular.

But the moment they arrived at Genius, the evening took a turn for the worse. She hadn't expected Eric to select this restaurant, but why wouldn't he? It was trendy and popular, frequented by celebrities. He may have seen pictures of her here with Cope, but Eric wouldn't know this was where she'd had her first lunch date with the former limo driver.

Flashbulbs popped and voices called her name. Her hand tucked into the crook of her date's arm, Dani walked toward the building's entrance without pausing. She wiggled her fingers in greeting at the fans who called to her and ignored the reporters.

The couple stepped into the restaurant's darkness, and when her eyes recovered from the camera flashes and adjusted to the low light, she scanned the dining room. And there he was: Cope—with a date.

Dani's heart drooped and sorrow overwhelmed her when he lifted his head and met her gaze. His eyes betrayed surprise, then they widened in shock when he registered Eric next to her. The woman with him— Katherine, his old friend, Margaret's favorite—leaned over, laid a hand on his shoulder, and murmured in his ear.

That broke the eye-lock Dani and Cope had established, and she wondered how long her prison term would be if she went over and slugged the bimbo.

"Is everything okay?" Eric said.

Dani realized she was holding her breath and exhaled with a small sigh. "Yes, everything's fine. Why?"

Before he could reply, Francois, the maître d' appeared and, recognizing Dani, welcomed them. "Please, follow me. I have the perfect table."

"I made a reservation," Eric said.

"Yes, sir," Francois replied. "This way."

She smiled what she hoped was a radiant smile and threw a glance in Cope's direction, but averted her eyes when his gaze once again met hers. Focused on following the headwaiter, she kept her hand on Eric's arm.

When they were seated, Eric took her hand. "Are you uncomfortable?"

"No. Why?" She played dumb, not sure if he knew she'd spotted Cope. Self-conscious with Eric's hand on hers, she forced herself not to snatch her hand from his. If it bothered Cope, what did it matter? She had as much right to be out with another man as Cope had to be out with another woman. But did it have to ache so much?

"Your ex-boyfriend is here. Sorry, Dani. I didn't expect him to be here."

"It's okay. How could you have known?" She extricated her hand from his and flipped the menu open, scanned it, and wondered what she could order that would stay down. The sight of Cope with that woman had made her lose her appetite.

A salad. She'd order a salad and mineral water. That, at least, should land in her stomach without wanting a return trip. The waiter appeared and took their order, and then Dani attempted to take an interest in her date.

"How's the marketing business doing?"

"It's going well. I've just landed a new client."

Eric worked for a PR firm doing Internet marketing and had done well for himself. He'd worked his way up from a junior position and was now director of sales. A long-haired woman requesting an autograph interrupted their discussion. Dani scribbled her name on a piece of paper.

Francois appeared and confronted the fan. "I'm sorry, ma'am, but we frown on customers disrupting meals to get autographs from celebrities here. Please return to your table."

The woman blushed and hurried away.

Francois turned to Dani. "My apologies, Miss Grayson. I'll see that it doesn't happen again. Security will keep a closer watch on your table."

"Thank you," Dani said.

Francois nodded and left.

She smiled at Eric. "They're great at controlling that here, but sometimes, someone slips past. Security knows, and they take care of me. Sorry for the interruption."

"It's not your fault," he replied. "It goes with the territory. Must frustrate sometimes."

A raised voice caught her attention, and she turned her head in the direction from which it came.

Cope argued with a woman. He'd headed toward Dani's table, and security had intervened. His indignant voice reached her ears.

"I'm not just a fan. We're friends, and I have a right to speak to her."

He stepped around the woman trying to hold him back and approached the table. Face flushed, frown distorting his handsome features, and hands fisted, he looked as if he wanted to slug something.

Dani glanced at the date he'd left behind at his table. Katherine's gaze followed Cope as he strode to Dani's side. The stunned concern on the blonde's face made Dani smug and guilty at the same time.

Security followed Cope, looking questioningly at Dani, who waved her hand to indicate it was okay.

The woman nodded and said, "I'll be nearby if you need me, Miss Grayson." She resumed her position at the side of the room.

"Cope?" Dani said when he reached the table.

"Where's Ryan Pearlman?" he said through gritted teeth.

He'd fought his way to her table to ask about the bodyguard?

"I don't know."

"What do you mean you don't know?"

"Go back to your date. I came with Eric tonight. And I don't answer to you."

Eric spoke up then. "Miss Grayson and I are on a date." He looked at Dani. "Want me to call security back?"

She met Eric's gaze and shook her head. "No, I'm sure Mr. Copeland was just leaving." She turned back to Cope. "If you think we have something to discuss, call me tomorrow. Otherwise, your date's getting annoyed."

Face flushed with fury, Cope turned on his heel and returned to his table. When he sat, he looked over at Dani again, and she felt her insides churn at the obvious pain in his eyes.

The waiter arrived with their drinks, setting a mineral water with lime in front of Dani and a glass of beer in front of Eric. When the server left, she gave Eric a weak smile. "I'm sorry for that, too."

"Again, that wasn't your fault. Let's try to make the best of it. I'm sure he won't bother you anymore. You've made your position clear."

The waiter arrived with their food, and Dani picked at the arugula salad while Eric feasted on steak, potatoes, and mixed vegetables. Throughout the meal, she stole glances at Cope's table.

His date no longer looked shaken, but rather appeared to be having the time of her life. To Dani, the woman's gestures of affection toward Cope and bursts of giggles seemed contrived. A knot of jealousy formed in Dani's stomach at the sight. She remembered, in painful detail, the wonderful times she'd spent with Cope, both here and at their respective apartments.

She tried not to recall the picnic on the beach. Her heart hurting, she gazed into her salad, picked up a single leaf with her fork, and nibbled on it.

"Dani?" Eric said gently. "Are you okay?"

"Yes. I'm sorry. I guess I wasn't paying attention."

"You've barely touched your salad."

She stared at her plate. "It's delicious." She took another forkful and chewed it slowly.

"Why don't we leave?" he suggested. "We can go to my place where it's not so distracting."

Not sure how to respond to that, she glanced again at Cope's table. The two had finished their meal and were enjoying coffee and dessert. One plate. Two forks.

Dani's breath caught in her throat, and her stomach threatened to reject the arugula she'd just swallowed. "I'd love to get out of here. Okay. Let's go to your place. Finish your dinner, and we'll leave."

"I'm done. Sorry, but I should've insisted on leaving when I saw your reaction to Copeland's presence. I've lost my appetite too." For the first time since they'd arrived, Eric showed irritation at the situation.

She flushed and lowered her gaze, unable to meet his eyes.

"I'm not mad at you. I don't know what happened between you and Copeland, other than what I've read or heard in the press, but he was crazy to let you go. Now you're not with him, he had no right to intrude on our date." He signaled the waiter and asked for the bill.

Tempted to check on Cope again, she forced herself to focus on Eric. They chatted while they waited for the server to return, and she concentrated on comprehending everything he said. At one point, he took her hand, which rested on the table, and held it. Her gaze jumped to Cope, who caught her glance and frowned at her.

Eric released her hand when he noticed where she was looking. "Maybe it's too soon for you to be going out with someone else." The irritation was back in his voice.

"I'm so sorry. His presence makes me self-conscious. I'll be all right away from here. I promise." At least, she hoped she'd be all right once they left the restaurant. Obligation made her want to stay with Eric and salvage the evening though her heart ached. What she wanted was to go home, curl up in bed, and cry.

By the time Eric paid the bill, Dani's nerves had frayed to a ragged edge, and it took concerted effort not to bolt out of the restaurant. Finally, Eric stood and offered her his arm. She rose and, grasping the proffered arm lightly with one hand, she let him lead her to the door. With every step she fought the urge to see what Cope was doing, what his date was doing.

None of my business. But how could he have moved on when he'd never even allowed her to explain her side of what had happened? She'd asked herself that at least a hundred times since he'd walked out on her and pondering it escalated the hurt.

A crowd on the street greeted them as they stepped onto the sidewalk. Dani cringed and huddled against Eric while the mob pressed in around them. He put an arm around her, protected her, while they waited for the valet to get the car.

Camera flashes exploded around them, and she wondered how Cope would react to seeing her nestled against Eric. Afraid it would make Cope abandon her forever, she wanted to step away from Eric, but the press of people around them froze her to the spot. Relieved to see the car at last, she allowed him to help her into the passenger seat.

Eric's apartment turned out to be near hers, and, though followed by paparazzi, they arrived in less than twenty minutes. Silent through the ride up in the elevator, she wondered how long she'd have to stay before she could go home. The doors slid open on the fourth floor, and the two stepped into the hallway, Eric reaching for her hand. She let him take it, and they walked to his unit still in silence.

The door opened onto a large, one-bedroom apartment, sparsely furnished. "I haven't decorated much since I moved in. I guess I'm waiting for the right woman's touch."

At those words, her head snapped around, and she stared, wide-eyed, at him.

"Relax, Dani. I'm not implying anything. Have a seat, and I'll make coffee or tea. Which do you prefer?"

"Tea please. I'll help you." That would give her something to do, and at least he wasn't trying to get her to drink alcohol now they were in his apartment. Was Cope taking Katherine back to his place now? Were they going to sleep together?

Oh, God, I can't do this. I have to get out of here.

She couldn't leave yet. They hadn't even sat down. Dani asked Eric where the teapot was while he filled the kettle. This would be a long night.

CHAPTER 27

Dani and her date walked out the door, and Cope fought the urge to run after them. He wasn't sure what he'd do if he caught up to them. It was a tossup between grabbing Dani and kissing her until her knees buckled or slugging the date in the face until *his* knees buckled. What if he was taking her back to his place? The thought of Dani, vulnerable and hurting, going to another guy's apartment made Cope's insides churn.

He finished a last sip of coffee and signaled the waiter for the check. "Sorry, Kate. I can't stay here."

Katherine brushed Cope's cheek with her fingers. "You have it bad, my friend. You won't try to follow them, will you? They're long gone by this point."

"No, but I might just sit in her apartment building until she gets home."

"Oh, Cope. Stalking?" She sucked in a breath through gritted teeth. "That's not needy."

"I can live without the sarcasm." She was right though. But the days without Dani had been hell, and the more time passed, the more miserable he became.

"Why continue to punish her? And don't launch into all that blah, blah, blah about your pride and respect. I'm not discounting your feelings, but why haven't you at least heard her out?"

Why indeed? He'd wanted to call Dani a hundred times since he'd left her. Part of it was he felt like a heel for abandoning her. "Shame. I'm ashamed I left her after she'd just been traumatized. But I was so angry. I thought she was manipulating me to get what she wanted."

Katherine sighed. "Since then, you wallow every time we get together. You must face her sometime. Didn't you see how badly she's hurting?"

"Yeah. She's hurting so badly she's on a date with another man."

Katherine laughed. "You're on a date with another woman."

"No, I'm not."

"For God's sake, Dani doesn't know that. Did you notice her face when she spotted us together? She could've killed me with that look. Did you ever tell her I'm gay?"

His head snapped around to face Katherine. "No. It's not my place to out you to anyone."

"That's considerate of you, darling, but what do you suppose Dani thinks when she sees our picture splashed all over the papers? Now she's seen us here together, it's even worse for her."

"She knows you and I are just friends. I told her that." His hands went cold, and his stomach knotted. The thought of Dani believing he'd moved on sickened him. What if it compelled her to find someone else?

"She's an insecure young woman, struggling to overcome childhood trauma, rape, and an assault. Her assumption will be that you're over her and going back to your first love. God, Rob, you can be such a fucking man."

The waiter appeared, and they stopped talking while he paid the bill. When they were alone again, Cope stood and pulled Katherine to her feet. "Let's go. I'll drop you at your apartment. I just hope it's not too late."

***

Dani stuck it out at Eric's until twelve-thirty. She'd relaxed as the evening wore on, and by the time she left, she no longer felt as if she'd hung around just to be polite. While he didn't make her heart sing, the two had spent a pleasant few hours chatting and watching a movie. What she appreciated the most was he didn't pressure her to get more intimate than she was comfortable with.

While the movie played, he'd put his arm around her, and she'd rested her head on his shoulder. They'd kissed, but it was friendly rather than passionate. After the movie, Dani called for a cab, and Eric walked her down to the lobby.

"Thank you. I had a nice time. Sorry dinner didn't go well. I'll make it up to you." She smiled.

He returned the smile, eyes showing affection. "No worries. Can we do it again? I promise I'll pick a different restaurant."

"Okay. I'd enjoy that." He was nice—good company. It wouldn't be terrible to spend time with him sometimes though he couldn't fill the void Cope had left in her life. That might never be filled, but eventually, she'd get used to living with it.

Lighter than she'd felt in a long time, she climbed into the cab and headed home.

***

Dani paid the cab driver and stepped out of the vehicle, careful to keep her short skirt from rising up and her high heels from tripping her. The warm, humid air hugged her as she walked to the building's entrance.

Silence, except for the sound of the odd car driving by on the street, blanketed everything. Street grime mixed with the floral perfume of landscaped gardens scented the air. No reporters or fans hung around outside the building. It was after one in the morning.

A man stepped from the lobby onto the sidewalk, the familiar form making the breath catch in her throat.

"Cope." She halted though he held the door open.

"We need to talk. Can we go up to your apartment?"

She studied him. His expression was wary.

"Why didn't you call or text me? I'd have come home earlier."

"Not here, Dani, please. Let's go inside."

"How'd you get in? I should move. Security here is terrible." She brushed past him.

That made him smile. "I begged them not to throw me out. Wave when you pass the cameras to let the guys know you're okay, or they'll come running."

She realized she was trembling and stepped carefully, mindful of the spike heels. Instinct and familiarity made her want to reach out and take his arm, but she fought the urge. Cope didn't look as though he wanted to return to the familiar or intimate.

The distance between them brought tears to her eyes. All she wanted to do was put her arms around him, fall into his embrace, and kiss him with every ounce of passion she could muster.

While they waited for the elevator, her palm twitched with the need to take his hand. She clasped her hands together and stared at the doors in front of her.

"Where's the bodyguard, Daniella?"

She whipped her head around to face him. "Tell me that's not why you're here."

"No, it isn't," he admitted. "But you came home in a cab. Where's your driver? Where were you?"

"Robert—" The elevator's arrival interrupted, and she stepped inside, Cope following close behind her. If they had this discussion now, she'd say something she'd regret, and it would drive the wedge between them deeper. She clamped her lips together and pressed the button for the penthouse. The doors slid shut. The numbers flashed at each floor, and she stared at the sequence as if it were the most fascinating thing she'd ever seen.

"It's not safe for you to be out without the bodyguard. Why didn't you take the limo?"

"Eric picked me up, and we went out for dinner."

"You left the restaurant. Obviously, you didn't come home right away."

The elevator stopped, and Dani led Cope to her unit, anger rising the closer they got to her home. Cope had left her, refused to speak to her, and now he showed up in the middle of the night after he'd seen her with another guy.

If there was a God, seeing her with Eric had ripped Cope's heart out as much as it had killed her to see him with Katherine. Yes, it was immature. *The hell with maturity.* She wanted karma to bite him in the ass since it had taken such a big chunk out of her own butt.

Dani unlocked the apartment door and stepped inside. Behind her, Cope shut and locked it.

When she turned to face him, his gaze traveled up and down her body. "You look nice."

"Thank you. What do you want—other than to inform me I should use a bodyguard when I leave my apartment? Consider the suggestion under advisement. Now, tell me why you're here instead of with your date." The trembling in her body and ache in her heart grew fiercer.

Was he here because he wanted to reconcile?

She kicked off the spike heels and walked to the couch to sit before her legs gave out. A yearning to have his arms around her, his body on top of her, brought her close to tears. She bit her lip to stem the tide while he stared in silence.

"Cope?" Her voice was gentle, and she couldn't keep the longing out of it.

"I had to see you. Since I left you, I've been in agony." He sat down next to her, making her heart pound.

She licked her lips. "Why didn't you let me explain? You may not have agreed with my justifications, but you could at least have heard me out. I loved you, Robert." Past tense. Too afraid to say it in the present tense. It might be too late for that.

He smiled when she said his name and then shook his head in such a sorrowful way it tore at her. "You rarely call me by my proper name—only when you're emotional over something. Or ..." He trailed off, probably not wanting to say "when we make love."

She lowered her eyes, afraid he'd notice the hovering tears. "Robert." It slipped out again, on its own, ache, need, hurt, and despair coating it.

His arms went around her, crushing her. When his mouth covered hers, she threw her arms around him and gripped him tight, pressing against him with her whole body. The tears coursed down her face and a sob escaped. When he removed his lips from hers, she gasped in fear, but he kissed away the tears and the loneliness.

"Oh, God, I'm so sorry. I should have let you explain. Whatever you intended, I should have trusted you. When I saw you with that guy tonight, it felt like someone had shoved a hot poker into my heart."

Pressing her head against his chest, Dani squeezed him tighter. Cope's body shook and, disbelieving, she looked up to confirm that he was crying.

"The woman you were with—Katherine." She couldn't continue.

"I'm sorry. It must've crushed you. I was so confused, so angry, and hurt. I tried to wipe you out of my mind, but don't get the wrong idea about Katherine."

They clung to one another on the couch. Both had stopped crying, and Cope stroked Dani's hair in that way he'd always done.

"Did you sleep with her?" She gasped as soon as the words left her mouth. "Sorry. It's none of my business."

"It's okay. The answer's no. We're just friends. I never wanted to hurt you, and I don't want to be without you. When the media referred to me as 'sugar baby' and 'kept man,' I felt emasculated and humiliated. I blamed you for what they'd done when I should have shrugged it off and ignored it."

Dani kept her hands on him—running fingers through his hair, stroking his cheek, or pressing on his chest. It assured her he was here, he was real, and he wouldn't disappear forever.

"Oh, God." It choked out of her. The thought of Cope disappearing called to mind her father, and she gagged on the horror of what had happened to him.

"What is it?" Cope's face had gone white, and his expression registered concern.

She shook her head. "It's okay. It's just … what happened to my father … I still have the dreams. You left me, and I was afraid you were gone forever, and would see me only in the magazines or on the news." Cope *had* seen her in the media, and it had pushed him away from her.

"I'm so sorry. I didn't intend to cause you pain, just protect myself and my pride. My family hounded me to use their money, wanting to control everything. I assumed you were doing the same thing, which was unfair. I'm ready to listen to your side of it now. Tell me what happened."

So she explained that, to make it up to him for getting him fired, she'd asked William to keep an eye out for Cope's proposal. "You submitted it without my interference, and Star Power informed me when it arrived. William said he'd have granted you an interview based on the proposal's merits even if I hadn't asked him to watch for it."

Dani paused and took one of Cope's hands in hers, turned it over, and traced a finger along the life line. When she raised her eyes to check if he was angry with her again, he hugged her tighter and kissed the top of her head.

"I'm not mad anymore. Keep going. Tell me the truth now, so I can set up a defense against the press. They'll continue with this 'sugar baby' bullshit when they know we're back together. I can live with it as long as I know that's false."

When they know we're back together. Music to her ears though a devil on her shoulder made her want to tell him not to decide for her. She released the toxic thought and carried on with her story. "You presented your case to the execs. I observed, which isn't unusual, though I don't watch every prospect present." Chin jutting out, she said, "It's my right as the owner of the company to view whatever presentations catch my interest, and you were special. I had to see it."

"I understand. The problem was you did it behind my back without telling me you were involved. That's what hurt. But one thing at a time. Go on."

"The feedback was positive. They all wanted to back you, except Nate, and apparently, he has a history with your father. I told them I wanted to fund you, but that if they didn't consider it viable, I'd defer to their decision. They were in favor of it. You landed this on your own. The result would've been the same even if I'd stayed out of it."

"But you didn't tell me you owned that company. You tracked the entire process and celebrated with me when I got the funding but didn't tell me it was yours. It made me think you didn't respect me or trust me and you wanted to control me. The capper was hearing about it on the news."

"I'm so sorry. I don't know how else to say it. My intention was to help you—make it up to you for causing you to lose your job. It always comes back to that because it consumed me. I wanted to tell you so many times, but I was afraid."

He turned his face away from her, and it made her heart jump in fear. He spoke, staring off into nothing. "I abandoned you, and I'm a shit for doing it. I've been miserable ever since I walked out on you, leaving you to handle an attempted rape without me. My beauty, I'm the one who needs to ask for forgiveness."

The reference to his pet name for her overwhelmed her. "I don't want to keep going without you, Cope. If I have to, I will, but I don't want to. I went out with Eric to fill the empty hours and because he's a nice guy."

She answered his unspoken question. "We didn't sleep together. It would be a long time before I could accept someone else into my bed after what you and I had together."

Cope's fingers played with her hair, and she leaned into him, let him cradle her against his shoulder. The stress eased out of her, and she sighed.

"Daniella," he whispered. "I want you. I need you. Can we take this to your bedroom?"

CHAPTER 28

Silently, Dani pressed her lips to Cope's, and after a long, deep kiss, pulled away. She nodded—just a slight tilt of her head—once, twice. He stood, clasped her hand, and helped her off the couch. Suddenly shy, she took reassurance from his warm palm against hers.

In the bedroom, Dani unbuttoned Cope's shirt and slid it off his arms. "God, how I've missed your beautiful body."

One of his fingers traced the outline of her lips, and then, gentle and loving, he bent his head to kiss her again. His mouth moved from her lips and glided over her cheek to her throat where it lingered while he nibbled and tasted. Her breath came in gasps, and the room wavered around her. Her hands clasped around his neck, she tingled at his every touch.

A nip on her ear made her groan. He drew down the zipper on the back of her dress. She helped by unclasping her arms and wiggling out of the cotton shift, letting it puddle at her feet. He nuzzled between her breasts, and when he unhooked her bra, she dropped her arms again and let that slide to the floor as well.

"I want you on that bed. Now." His voice grew hoarse, laced with desire.

Dani drew away from him, turned back the covers, and climbed onto the bed. Draped across the mattress in just her thong, she ran her hands over her body to settle the swelling ache. "Please, Robert. I need you on me."

An attempt to speak failed, and he let out a growl from deep in his throat. Shoes, pants, socks, and briefs hit the floor next to Dani's clothes, and then he was on her, pressing his body against her. One hand massaged her breast, then held it still while he took the nipple in his mouth and suckled, nipped, and teased.

Moans escaped, rising from the depths of her core, and she writhed under him. The sweet agony was so strong she thought she might pass out. Her hand reached between them, and she yanked her panties off, ignoring the tearing sound that accompanied the motion. The throbbing between her legs intensified. If he didn't enter her soon, she'd scream from the unbearable need.

His hand moved along her body and between her legs, probing and exploring, making her cry out.

"Please. Please. Please." Brain fogged, she stroked her hands over his biceps and his back. Did he ache as much as she did? The groan spilling from his lips made her believe he did.

"Daniella." He kissed her again, tongues tangling, anticipation building. He fiddled with a condom, and she wanted to howl in frustration at the time it took to slide it on.

"Oh, Robert, now." She guided him to the soft entrance she wanted him to penetrate. Urgency pushed her pelvis into him. So long. She'd been so horribly long without him inside her. She arched her back, pressed against him, spreading her thighs wider in welcome.

His own need obliged, and he thrust into her, hard, their movements growing more frenzied with the contact. Cries mingling, they gave to each other, filling the voids that had opened during their separation. Dani never wanted to be apart from him again, and her whole body gripped him, caressed him, and loved him.

"Deeper. Please, I need you, all of you." Unaware she'd said that aloud, the rolling wave of passion consumed her, brought her to the edge, and flung her over. Uncontrolled moans and sighs ripped from her throat, and Cope's thrusts became fiercer as his own climax followed hers. She tightened her internal muscles, drawing a moan of pleasure from him.

"Oh, God, Dani, you're killing me."

She sighed, contented, and hugged him tight when he collapsed on top of her. "I could stay this way forever."

He let out an exhausted breath. "You're wonderful. That was amazing." He groaned. "I need to move though. Are you okay?"

She nodded, and he rolled onto his back, pulling her into the shelter of his arm as he did. Head on his shoulder, she stroked his soft skin with one hand, a slow, lazy gesture that reflected the sultry ambience of the room. Kisses—lots of kisses—covered his face, shoulders, and chest.

One of Cope's hands reached out to brush hair off Dani's face. He turned to her, gazed into her eyes, and smiled. "I love you."

Dani returned the smile. "I love you, too."

Afraid that anything said after that would ruin the moment, she snuggled against him and allowed herself to drift into a contented sleep.

***

Voices. Loud, argumentative. A man and a woman. Father. Mother. Dani listened from her bedroom. The memories returned in a lightning bolt flash. In the darkness of her apartment bedroom, Dani's mind turned back to the room she'd had as a five-year-old child. Back to that night. It burst into her consciousness when she awoke, Cope's warm body anchoring her, making her feel safe and protected.

At last, she knew what had happened, understood what she'd seen. The horror of it made her wrench up in the bed, pulling the sheet with her. She paused and gently tucked it back over his chest.

For a moment, she listened to his light snoring, loving the manliness of the sound. If history were any indicator, there'd be times when it wouldn't sound so appealing, and he'd get a poke and a request to roll over. In the dim glow of the clock radio, she watched him sleep, letting the sight of his beautiful, innocent face ground her and squeeze out the terror.

She'd have to call Detective Vega. A glance at the clock showed that while it was early here, in Toronto the morning was well underway. It would be okay to call him now. She slipped out of bed, threw on her robe, and went to put on the coffee.

Once it was brewing, she walked into the living room and retrieved her purse from the floor. It astounded her that so little time had passed since she'd dropped it there. So much had happened since Cope had greeted her downstairs after her date with Eric.

Eric. She'd promised him she'd go out with him again. Heat from a flush crept up her face though no one was around to judge her except herself. Dani shook her head. *Can't think about Eric now. Have to call Vega.* She'd call Eric after and tell him she and Cope were back together before he read it in the news.

Cell phone now in hand, she speed-dialed the detective and waited while the call transferred. He picked up on the second ring.

"Detective Vega? Daniella Grayson."

"Dani? How are you? What can I do for you?" His voice was warm, friendly. It had been a while since they'd last spoken, but he always seemed happy to hear from her whenever she called.

"I'm fine. Great, in fact. I remembered, Detective—the whole night." Voice low, but excited, Dani wanted to pour her story out though the recollections were disturbing.

"I'll record this, okay?"

"Yes."

"Give me a moment."

She waited while Vega set up the recording device, and stated the date, time, his name, and had Dani give her name.

"Okay. Start from the earliest memory of that evening and tell me everything."

She curled up on the couch and spoke. "My father put me to bed and left my room to go watch TV. Lilli immediately nattered at him, telling him he needed to find work. Daddy replied he was doing his best, but she said that wasn't good enough. She must've stood in front of the television, blocking his view, because Daddy told her to move out of the way."

She paused. "My father rarely raised his voice or got angry, but even he had a breaking point. After days of being home with Lilli picking at him, he snapped."

When she paused again, Vega interjected. "What were you doing?"

"Cowering in my bed. I knew it'd get worse—maybe bad enough for Lilli to hit him. People think spousal abuse victimizes women, but men can be abused too. My mother belittled Daddy. She cursed him out, threw things at him, and even hit him. Daddy put up with it because he didn't want to leave. Anytime he threatened to walk out and take me along, she taunted him, calling him a loser. No judge would award him custody, she said, and he had no one to take care of me when he went to work."

Tears welled up. Hearing a sound behind her, she turned toward it. Cope walked around the couch to her side.

"One moment, Detective." She pulled the phone away from her ear. "I remember, Robert."

"Shall I leave the room while you talk?"

She shook her head. "I'm glad you're here."

While Cope settled next to her, Dani returned her attention to Vega. "Sorry, Detective. That night, the fighting escalated, and before long, it turned to accusations of cheating."

"Who accused whom?"

"Both of them. Lilli told Daddy she thought he was cheating on her. Daddy said that was the pot calling the kettle black if he ever saw it. She laughed at him and said that she didn't care if he knew she was, she was ..." It was difficult to say the words.

Cope took her free hand and held it in both of his.

Dani gulped in air, swallowed her tears, and continued. "She admitted to cheating on him. I didn't understand what it meant, but I knew it involved Daddy's friend. Then Daddy told her he hadn't slept with anyone else, but he was leaving, and taking me with him. Lilli said, 'The hell you will. Try to take my baby from this house, I'll kill you.' "

A squeeze on Dani's hand made her glance up at Cope. She searched his eyes and saw compassion. Vega waited on the other end, silent.

"Thank you, Detective."

"For what?"

"For being so patient with me."

"I know how hard this must be for you. Continue whenever you feel able."

Steadied, she spoke again. "I was relieved that Daddy wanted to take me away from the shouting and the hitting. The stress of trying not to make Lilli mad, day after day, and failing was unbearable. When Daddy mentioned leaving, I got out of bed and tiptoed from the bedroom. If they saw me, they'd be angry, so I tried to be quiet. I got as far as the living room entrance. Lilli chose that moment to come charging out into the hallway, and she caught me. I peed myself when she rounded the corner and walked into me."

A glance at Cope again reassured her, and she stared off into space, letting the story flow out of her. "Lilli grabbed me by the ear." The memory gave Dani an echo of pain on her left ear, making her flinch. "She screamed at me, which wasn't unexpected, and she hit me, which was also not unexpected. Lilli called me a little pig and told me I had to clean up my filthy mess. I cried, so afraid of her I couldn't move. Daddy came into the hallway and told Lilli to leave me alone. He said, 'She's just a child, Lilli. I'll clean it up.' He told me to go change into a dry nightgown and everything would be okay because we were leaving."

"That was the last time I saw Daddy." Voice breaking, she wished for a shot of vodka. Another glance at Cope helped the urge to pass. "I went to my room, Lilli right behind me. I changed into another nightgown, and when I tried to get into bed, she grabbed me and ..."

Cope pulled Dani into his arms, held her while she sobbed.

Vega's voice spoke in her ear. "It's okay, Dani. It's all right. Continue when you're ready."

Still sobbing, she choked out more of the story. "Lilli locked me in the closet. It was dark, and I was so scared. She didn't say a word—just grabbed me and threw me in there and locked the door. Oh, God, I was just a scared little kid. I thought she was mad because I'd wet myself, and this was my punishment, but I think she was already thinking about killing him.

"She left me in that closet the entire night. I slept there—tried to, anyway. In the morning, she got me to school. When I came home from kindergarten, she told me Daddy had left. She said he didn't want to take me with him. It broke my heart. I always wondered what I'd done that made him leave me behind, that maybe he didn't want me because I'd peed myself. But she'd lied." In a quiet voice, she said, "Daddy didn't leave me behind." Dani finished with a loud sigh, relieved at getting the story out.

Vega thanked her for calling and told her he'd have to fly out to LA to interview her again. "I'll need to video record it for the trial. It's great you got it all out while it was fresh in your mind, but I need an in-depth interview."

She agreed and told him she'd have her assistant set it up. They said their goodbyes and disconnected.

She turned to Cope. "Thank you for being here. I don't know how I'd have gotten through it by myself."

"I love you, Dani, and I'll always be here for you." He kissed the top of her head. "So sorry you had to experience that. It must have been terrible to believe your father abandoned you and endure such abuse from your mother." His arms tightened around her, making her feel safe and secure.

This sense of stability had allowed the memories to come flooding back as Doctor Hadley had told Dani they would. Relieved she didn't have to go to work early, she suggested they have breakfast before Cope had to leave. With the grand opening of his business looming, he was working long hours every day of the week.

He headed to the shower, muttering about a meeting he had, while Dani went to the kitchen to prepare breakfast. Déjà vu hit her when she pulled ingredients out of the fridge to make a veggie omelet. The last time she'd wanted to make a meal for him, it had ended in disaster. Well, she'd leave the television off. If the news had anything to say regarding her or Cope, it could wait.

But when the phone rang, she answered it.

CHAPTER 29

Dani picked up the phone.

Liz cut off her hello. "Are you watching the news?"

Dani's heart sank. "No." Too afraid to ask what this was about, she waited for her friend to continue.

"He's out on bail."

"Greg?" Dani folded onto the couch.

"Yes. Turn on the TV. It's all over the news. There was a problem, or they'd have released him the day after his arrest. He has to stay with his parents until the case goes to court and the verdict comes back. I wanted to make sure you're okay."

Dani glanced toward the hallway, but saw no sign of Cope. "I'm fine. Cope's here. We're back together." Her voice rose with excitement when she said the words.

"Oh, I'm so happy for you guys. You're so great together. He needs to hear about this. I feel better knowing he's with you."

"Greg won't come near me now. He's not crazy."

"No, but if he's drinking, he's dangerous. Let Cope know. Promise?"

"Yes, I'll tell Cope."

"Tell me what?" Cope appeared, hair damp and dressed in his clothes from the previous night.

Dani thanked Liz for the information and ended the call. She went to him and hugged him.

"What's wrong?"

"Greg's out on bail." She told him everything.

He cursed and pressed her tight against his chest. "You go nowhere without Ryan."

Not surprised he led with telling her to use the bodyguard, she nevertheless resented the delivery. "Is that an order?"

He pulled back and stared into her eyes. "If it keeps you safe, take it however you like. That bastard is out on the streets, and I doubt the short incarceration cured his alcohol problem. Ryan's driving you to the studio this morning, right?"

"It's a location shoot today, but yes, he should be here soon." She remembered the omelets warming in the oven. "Let's eat. Don't worry. I'll make sure Ryan's around when you're not, Sir Knight." She smiled and pulled him to the kitchen table.

Two hours later, in the on-location trailer that would be her dressing room for the next two weeks, Dani put on a robe, preparing for makeup. She still hadn't listened to the news, afraid to risk upsetting herself by seeing Greg's picture splashed all over the screen.

Paparazzi had camped outside her apartment again. When she'd left for work, Cope's presence turned their goodbye kiss into a photo frenzy. She wanted to avoid seeing those images too.

At least she'd be spending most of the day in this secluded mountain area. Preoccupied with the shoot, she'd be able to let the outside world stay outside. Dani looked over the outfit wardrobe had left for her: a business suit, and she'd be climbing rocks and running through brush in it. The stunt double would handle the risky stuff, but Dani would still get dirty, and scenes like this always contained an element of danger.

A knock on the door brought her out of thoughts of scaling cliffs and climbing trees. She let in the makeup artist, sat on the stool in front of the vanity, and started her work day.

***

Cope's intercom buzzed, and his receptionist's voice interrupted the perusal of a report he'd been working on for the last half-hour. "Yes, Angela?" He glanced at the clock. Almost noon.

"Your mother is here to see you, Mr. Copeland."

His mother? What was she doing here? She'd never mentioned visiting the city today. "Send her in, please."

The door opened, and Margaret walked into the office. Face tilting every which way, she scanned the room. "Nice. Quaint. If you'd have accepted our money, it would be more sumptuous, but this is okay." She moved to the chair in front of his desk and sat.

"Nice of you to drop by. If you'd told me you were coming to the office today, I'd have planned to take you to lunch. As it is, I'm having food delivered and working through."

"I was in the neighborhood."

He studied her expression, searching for irony, but she was serious. "You're never in this neighborhood. What's going on?"

"I saw disturbing footage on the news." She crossed her ankles and folded her hands over the clutch she'd set in her lap.

"What news was that?" His stomach sank. It must involve Dani, or Margaret wouldn't be here.

"About you and that little trollop you brought to our party. I thought that was over, but apparently, I was mistaken. Reporters caught you coming out of her apartment this morning after you spent the night there. Her other lover is out on bail."

Cope grimaced. "Henderson's not her other lover. Yes, we're back together. I love her, and nothing you say will change that. Accept it."

"Your father and I don't approve. She's not suitable for you, Bobby. Her mother is in prison, accused of murder. Her father couldn't hold a job. She's slept with who knows how many men—certainly she's been intimate with Greg Henderson. You see the kind of people she surrounds herself with? You're not like them. She'll cause trouble for you."

"I appreciate your concern, but I know what I'm doing."

"My dear son,"—Margaret stretched her hand across his desk, beseeching—"you think you're in love, but you're confusing that with lust. I don't want to interfere, but I can't stay quiet while you ruin your life. Why did you take money from her and not from us?"

He shook his head. "It's complicated. Don't worry about us. It doesn't matter that her family aren't billionaires or that her mother's in jail. I love Dani. It might not work out, but I love her, and I want to give it a chance. Let it be."

"Fine. But don't say I didn't warn you. You don't know her as well as you think. You'll see. Sorry we can't do lunch. Another time." She stood and walked to the door. Before she left, she turned back to Cope. "I hope you don't regret your decision to continue seeing that girl. But remember this: when she breaks your heart, I'll be there to help you."

When Margaret had left, Cope picked up his cell phone and sent Dani a text: *Hope you're having a good day. I love you.*

***

Eyes closed, Dani sat back in the limo, gripping a bottle of water. A week had passed, and they were still on location. Vega had been and gone, the interview going smoothly. As far as she was concerned, he'd pulled nothing new from her memories, but he'd insisted the exercise was necessary.

Today's shoot had been long and grueling. She slipped off her shoes and massaged her aching feet. Heels were fine for clubbing or at a restaurant, but having to spend the day in them in a mountain forest was insane.

In the movie, her character had been kidnapped and held in a mountain cabin. While they shot the interior scenes in a studio, they shot outdoor scenes on location. Weather and daylight, or lack of it, conspired to slow them down. This would be a long week.

Dani's cell phone beeped, and she pulled it out and checked the incoming message. *Cope.* They were supposed to meet at a restaurant for dinner, but he was running late. Dani replied: *Come to my place when you're done. I'll fix something and we'll chill.*

He returned her text with a smiley face and a promise to be at her place for 8:30 PM, giving her three hours to prepare. Relieved they'd be spending a quiet evening at home, but surprised by that relief, she relaxed. When the phone went off again, she glanced at the call display and saw *Copeland.* Confused—it wasn't Cope's ringtone playing—she answered it.

"Cope?"

"It's Mrs. Copeland, Miss Grayson."

Dani's mouth went dry. "What can I do for you?"

"We need to meet."

"Why?"

"Come to my house tomorrow after work, and we'll talk."

"Does Cope know you want to see me?" Dani heard a sharp intake of breath.

"You won't want to discuss this with Bobby."

The line went dead.

Goodbye. Have a nice day. Dani's hands shook as she put her cell phone away.

CHAPTER 30

The next day, Dani went home to prepare for her meeting with Margaret. To make sure Cope wouldn't look for her, she'd told him she'd be having a late night and would call him when she got home. He asked no questions, trusting her, which gave her a stab of guilt.

Racks of clothes surrounded her, and she didn't know what to wear. Was this a business meeting? A battle for her boyfriend? What? In the end, she selected a simple cotton sheath dress that grazed her knees and a pair of flat sandals. Not wanting to have a record of her visit on Cope's books, she called a cab to take her to the Copeland estate.

The drive over found her biting her lip and clenching her fists until her fingernails dug into her palms. Blessed with a wild imagination, Dani pictured various crazy scenarios, half of them ending in her death, the other half ending with her killing in self-defense. She hoped Margaret didn't own a gun.

The sun was setting by the time she stood at the Copeland's front door. She'd talked herself into believing that the meeting would be something positive—perhaps a surprise party for Cope. That calmed her nerves enough to generate the courage required to ring the doorbell, which echoed through the house. She listened for approaching footsteps. Everything remained quiet.

A flutter in her stomach pushed thoughts of celebrations and joyful occasions out of her head. Hand shaking, she pressed the doorbell again, and before the chimes faded away, the door swung open.

Margaret stood before her dressed for tennis in a white and navy collared shirt, navy skirt, and white tennis shoes. Hair pulled back in a ponytail, accentuating her Botox-smooth skin and facelift, she resembled an aging coed.

Dani took a step backward and gulped in air, heart pounding. "Mrs.

Copeland. Hello." It came out in a breathy whisper. Cope would have thought it seductive.

"Yes. Well. Come in."

When Dani stepped inside, Margaret closed and locked the door, the sound of the deadbolt sliding into place sending a chill up Dani's spine. Margaret scurried down the hall, Dani trotting to keep up to her. They cut through the house, rushing past closed doors until they reached a massive kitchen that opened into a sunroom at the back of the house.

Margaret led the way through a set of sliding doors and into the garden. Lights illuminated the path through the manicured lawns, and the farther they walked, the more familiar became the route. They headed toward the gazebo where Dani and Cope had had their romantic interlude the night of the Copelands' big party.

Dani's knees trembled. What the hell was Margaret doing?

They reached the gazebo, and Margaret moved to the screened-in window on the west side, where Cope had shown Dani the view of the ocean. The breeze made her shiver, and she stole a glance at the loveseat where they'd lost themselves in passion.

"Familiar with this place, Miss Grayson?"

"Yes," she whispered.

"Scan the ceiling, along the walls. What do you see? Take a good look."

She raised her eyes and made a slow turn, following the line of the intersection of ceiling and wall. Cameras. Four of them. Who needed to film the inside of a gazebo from four different angles? The blood drained from her face and her stomach lurched.

"Care to watch the performance?" Margaret held up a phone, tapped the screen, and the video played, with sound.

Dani shivered, hands and feet growing cold. She heard their love talk, their moans and sighs. It sounded cheap and seedy floating up from the phone. She cringed when she heard herself say *I don't believe we're doing this. What if someone finds us out here?* And then Cope's flippant response: *In another few seconds, I won't care if they film it and post it to the Internet.*

"Stop this. Please." She couldn't bear to listen anymore, and she'd stopped watching the moment she realized what was on the screen. "Why would you do this?"

"Me? You're the one whoring around with my son."

"You must have spent quite a bit of time searching the video footage to find that."

Margaret's lips pressed into a thin line. "Not really. I watched the two of you leave. I figured he was taking you out here."

"So you spied on us? Why?"

"I had my reasons. What I found shocked me though. Now I have this evidence, perhaps we can come to an agreement?"

A lump had formed in Dani's throat, and she swallowed a few times. "What do you want?"

"What I've always wanted: you out of Cope's life."

Dani froze. "You're blackmailing me with this? What will you do? Show it to Cope? He's in it, Margaret." No more polite "Mrs. Copeland" bullshit. This woman had watched her have sex. If that didn't put them on a first-name basis, nothing did.

"Not at all. It's just more proof for me you're completely wrong for him. Does the name Cassandra Wilson ring a bell?"

It didn't. Dani shook her head.

"She remembers you. And Greg Henderson. The three of you were rather intimate after you and Henderson took her home with you from the restaurant where she worked."

A flash image of the waitress they'd had a three-way with jumped into Dani's head, and she swallowed around the large lump in her throat. "What relevance does she have to this conversation?"

"Henderson paid her off, but I offered her more to break her silence. This little story hasn't gone to the press yet, but it will if you don't agree to leave my son alone."

"So you're paying her to fabricate?"

"Not necessary. She filmed it with her cell phone, which means you can't act the innocent. You should learn to be more careful of whom you allow into your bed." Margaret tapped the phone again, and another video played.

Dani recognized her own voice and Greg's. Stomach in knots, she glanced at the screen. The three bodies in the bed tangled together, Dani in the middle, the other woman holding up an arm, taking a selfie. Nausea worked its way through Dani's intestines, and she fought the urge to throw up.

"Turn it off."

Margaret obliged, and the gazebo drenched in silence.

Dani broke it. "I love Robert. I'd never hurt him." Their recent fight about the investment company popped into her head. *Never again.* But she didn't vocalize it. His mother needed no extra ammunition.

"My fear isn't that you'll hurt him. This has little to do with his heart. I'm sure you think you love him. You're not right for him. Don't you see? You're not good enough for him." An ingratiating smile formed on her lips. It was as though she'd concluded her argument was so reasonable Dani must surely be ready to back down now, and the time to wrap up had arrived.

"Why am I not good enough? I've done things in my past I'm not proud of, but I've worked through all that. How can you judge me when you don't know me?"

The smile disappeared and Margaret frowned, puzzled. "What don't you understand? You and Bobby are from different worlds. Doubtless, you're a fun distraction—you're loose and give him whatever he wants sexually, but the difference in class will tear you apart. He'll want someone who can run his household and raise his children, and that won't be you."

Dani's hand itched to slap the ignorant woman. "I'm sorry. Did I wake up in the 1950s? Cope isn't sexist. He doesn't have a problem with me working, and he's seen me at my worst. It doesn't bother him."

"Perhaps. Let me put it in a way you might understand. If he continues to see you, he won't get any more support from this family. He'll be disinherited. We don't want to risk anyone undesirable getting their hooks into the family assets."

Dani opened her mouth to protest. She wanted nothing they had.

Margaret held up a hand and cut her off. "If you were to have kids, they'd inherit from him regardless of whatever contracts you might have signed. I don't want you or your future brats to be part of this family. You'll never be welcome here."

Close to tears and despair, Dani had one last arrow in her quiver. "Your husband and daughter don't agree with you. They were nice to me, accepting. Big Cope would never cut Robert off—he loves his son too much and wants him to be happy."

"How the hell do you know what Big Cope would do? Just because you bat your eyelashes at my husband you figure he'll side with you? He's not that easy." If Margaret had sneered or shouted, Dani could have told herself she'd touched a nerve and maybe she had a chance. But Margaret's tone was calm, conversational, and it chilled Dani.

"Consider how much you want to ruin Bobby's life. He'd be sorry to be saddled with you, and one day, he'll realize it. It'll happen even sooner if this video were to fall into the hands of the tabloids. How much more can he take? They're already calling him 'sugar baby' and 'kept man' because of you. Do you want to completely humiliate him?"

Tears threatened now, and Dani choked them back. *I'll be damned if I let this bitch break me.* "It wouldn't be me humiliating him; it would be you."

"No. The young lady would."

"Because of you!" Dani's voice pitched high, making Margaret smile.

"If Bobby were the only one to see it, what do you think he'd do then? Do you think he'd forgive you?"

"It's in my past. He wouldn't hold it against me. He's not like that."

"My dear, he'd know. That's all that's required to raise doubt, to make him wonder what kind of trashy woman he's involved with. Who knows how many times you've done this?"

Dani didn't reply. She thought it was just the once, but there were other nights when she'd awakened from a drunken stupor in bed with Greg and another person. Most of the time, it was another woman. Once, it was another man. She couldn't remember what had happened, and what if more footage turned up?

"How did you find Cassandra?" Surely, the waitress hadn't sought Margaret out. Then Dani understood. "You hired a private investigator."

The smirk on Margaret's face was answer enough. Without another word, Dani left the gazebo. She heard footsteps behind her, and then Margaret called out. "Miss Grayson."

Heart aching, Dani turned and faced Cope's mother.

Margaret's dead-fish gaze locked on Dani's. "Take the high road. Give Cope the life he deserves. Free him up to find someone suitable—someone who won't cause him embarrassment, who won't drag him down."

Dani turned away, pulled her cell phone from her purse, and called for a cab as she followed the winding path back to the front of the house.

CHAPTER 31

Working late again. So sorry I won't be able to see you today either.

Cope's shoulders sagged when he read the text message from Dani. For the third day in a row, they wouldn't be getting together. It crossed his mind she was pushing him out of her life, but then he shoved it aside. What reason would Dani have for avoiding him? If there was a problem with their relationship, she'd come to him with it.

Though uneasy, he texted back a quick *No worries, my beauty. We'll catch up tomorrow night.*

Tomorrow was Friday. She'd never worked so late on a Friday they couldn't get together. He turned his attention back to his work, reviewing the schedules for his drivers. He had five cars and eight drivers—all reliable men and women with martial arts training and licensed to conceal carry.

The phone rang, *Copeland* appearing on the call display.

He snatched it up and said, "Hello?"

"Bobby. How are you?"

"Fine, thanks, Mother. What's up?" He leaned back in his chair and stretched his legs out in front of him. Tension he hadn't realized he held released in his shoulders, back, and legs.

"Are you busy tonight? Come for dinner. Invite Dani. We haven't seen her since the night of the party."

"She's working late tonight." Cope sighed, blowing frustration into the mouthpiece.

"Something wrong?"

The concern in Margaret's voice was touching. She'd been so pushy about getting him and Katherine together it was refreshing to have her include Dani in dinner plans.

"No. She's just been busy for the last three days, and we haven't been able to get together. I miss her."

135

"Oh, what a shame. Come for dinner yourself, then. It'll give you something to do."

He considered his options. Nothing to do after work anyway, and it sure beat sitting at home missing Dani. Not the type to pine over a girlfriend, Cope chalked the angst up to the days he'd spent without her during their separation. It'd been his doing. What if she was avoiding him because she was afraid to get close to him again? *Stop it. She's just working late.*

"Okay. I'll be there."

"Wonderful." Enthusiasm bubbled over as she made him promise to arrive by seven o'clock that evening.

She seemed a little too empathetic about Dani's absence. Margaret never approved of the relationship, and as far as he knew, nothing had changed to make her grow fond of his girlfriend. Maybe Margaret loved him enough to consider his happiness. That thought made him smile. He didn't believe it for a minute.

Not that she didn't love him, but her obsession with only associating with the right people meant that accepting Dani into the family was a definite challenge for his mother. Cope had no illusions she'd accept the young actress unconditionally. Even so, he thanked Margaret for the dinner invitation and ended the conversation daring to hope that the two women might become friends.

***

Dani arrived home by six o'clock, and guilt made her ask Ryan to drive the limo into the underground parking to let her out. She doubted Cope would sit out there watching for her, but she didn't want to take the risk.

Once she was up in her apartment, she made herself a protein shake for dinner and sat on the couch to sip it while she waited for Liz to arrive.

Liz was filming two scenes in the *Injury* sequel at the studio. She had a speaking part, though it was a small one, and her character was killed off three-quarters of the way through the movie.

A beep from the cell phone signaled an incoming message, and Dani snatched it up.

Cope: *Sorry you can't have dinner with me. I'm heading to my parents' place. Don't work too late.*

She set down the phone. If she replied too quickly, he'd suspect she wasn't working.

A knot formed in her stomach and the protein shake suddenly didn't sit so well. She returned to the kitchen and teared up as she went through the motions of dumping the rest of the drink and washing the cup. For three days now, Margaret's words had made her avoid Cope.

An inability to decide whether to end the relationship or tell him his

136

mother was trying to break them up kept her from contacting him. She didn't want to give him up, but she also didn't want to hold him back. Was she an albatross around his neck as Margaret claimed? Would she end up making him miserable?

The ache in her heart had been constant, distracting her on the set. At least she could use that to her advantage since her character was grieving the loss of her partner and unable to focus.

But she was screwing up in other scenes, which meant extra takes. The location shoot would drag on longer than originally scheduled, and while not all of it was due to Dani's emotional state, she knew part of it was.

Liz arrived, Dani buzzed her in, and when the doorbell rang, she checked the peephole before opening the door.

"Are you okay? You look worried?" Liz hugged Dani.

At that, she burst into tears.

Liz led Dani to the couch, where she choked out her encounter with Margaret.

When she finished relaying the whole sordid story, she said, "What should I do? She's right. He's better off without me. I'm nothing but a burden to him."

She hung her head and the tears dripped unrestrained.

Liz took Dani's hands in hers. "Look at me."

She reluctantly raised her head and looked into her friend's eyes.

"You are a kind, loving, wonderful person, and any man would be lucky to have you. He loves you, and you love him. That should be reason enough for you to give it a chance."

"I want what's best for him."

"Why are you so damn sure that's not you?"

"Oh, God, I've done so many stupid things. How will I live it down?"

Liz was quiet for a moment. When she spoke, the words came out slow, but strong, as though she weighed each one.

"You know what you did. How do you live with it now? You're afraid that if what you did becomes public, you'll be so embarrassed you won't be able to … what? Leave the house? Make another movie? Live? Love? Be happy? Are you going to give strangers that much power over your life?"

Dani gave Liz a weak smile. "No. What'll Cope think of me when he finds out? He'll hate me."

"So to prevent something that might not happen, you'll preempt it by leaving him first?"

"When you put it that way, it sounds silly."

"That's because you're letting that Copeland bitch get into your head."

"You weren't there. She was brutal. She hates me because of who I am."

"It's amazing that she's got such a wonderful son."

"Yes, but what if she turns him against me?"

"Have you considered coming clean to him? If he knows, then if it gets out, he won't be shocked and he'll be there to support you. Besides, if he leaves you because of that, then you're better off without him, not the other way around."

Relief flooded through Dani. "You're right. See, that's why I hang out with you. You're the best girlfriend ever."

Liz laughed. "It'll be okay. Don't give your power to anyone. Now, let's practice our lines for tomorrow."

Dani smiled, feeling better than she had in days. She went to get the script and put the kettle on.

CHAPTER 32

When Cope walked in the door of his parents' place, Katherine was there to greet him. Happy to see her, but sensing Margaret's stratagem behind it, he kept things light and casual through dinner. After the meal, he escorted Katherine to the kitchen in the backyard and guided her to the large, rectangular table behind the marble-top island.

"You're aware my mother is trying to fix us up, right?"

Katherine pulled out a chair and sat while Cope went to the bar and fixed the drinks.

"Perhaps it's time I told her I'm seeing someone else?" Katherine said.

"If you did that, she'd want details. Are you ready to come out to my family? I'm sure my sibs will be okay with it, but my parents? Dubious."

"I'm a big girl. I can handle it. If she doesn't like who I am, it's not my problem. Are you okay with that? Because it sounds as if you're afraid to face your mother's prejudices."

"Sorry it came out that way." He poured a glass of red wine for Katherine and grabbed a beer from the fridge for himself. "I don't want her to make you unhappy. She can be controlling. We've grown up with it and have learned to deal, but you haven't seen her at her worst."

"Is she homophobic?"

He carried the drinks to the table and contemplated the question. "She hasn't expressed any hatred for gays, so probably not."

Katherine smiled. "What are you trying to protect me from? Bet you're afraid she'll stop pushing us together. Admit it. You have the hots for me, and you've been pining away all these years."

He laughed. "Okay, you got me." He paused and then continued. "You're right though. It's time we put an end to this charade. If you're okay with me outing you to my family and to Dani, then I'm okay with telling them."

At the thought of Dani, he frowned. He sat at the table next to Katherine and took her hand. "Not to change the subject, but I need relationship advice. Since you date women too, and you are one, perhaps you can help me?"

"Of course."

"Dani's avoiding me. I'm sure she is. She's telling me she's working late, which might be true, but she barely acknowledges my texts. Something has changed, made her pull away. I can feel it."

"You've got nothing concrete?"

"I understand how that sounds. But we went from seeing each other every night and texting throughout the day, to not seeing each other and me texting and her rarely responding."

"She's a busy actress." Katherine reached out a hand and stroked his face. "If I were attracted to men, it would've been easy for your mom to get us together. You're a great guy. Give the woman her space. She knows you're here for her. You're not worried she's found someone else?"

"No. That's ridiculous. When we split up, she was devastated." What if Dani was pulling back because she feared he'd leave her again? An urge to talk to her welled up, and he considered walking out and finding her, even if he had to track her down on location. He groaned. "You were right when you said I've got it bad."

The sound of the patio door sliding open made him look up. Margaret stepped outside and beamed a smile at them when her gaze landed on Cope's hands clasping Katherine's. He caught Katherine's eye, and she nodded, sliding her hand from Cope's.

"Oh, no, don't let me interrupt you two lovebirds."

"It's all right. We were just talking." Katherine beamed a return smile.

"There's something you should know, Mother."

Margaret walked to the bar and pulled out a bottle of scotch and a rocks glass. She poured two fingers for herself and returned the bottle to the cabinet.

"What's that, dear?" Her voice sounded hopeful, and her face brightened.

Shit. She was probably already planning their wedding. "Katherine was telling me about the person she met in college and plans to move in with."

Margaret's face fell, her jaw clenched, and the smile that appeared this time looked forced. "How delightful. Tell me about him."

"It's not a 'him.' It's a 'her.' Julie, my roommate in college. It turned out we had a lot in common, and before long, we fell in love. We were friends first, and living together at school drew us even closer together. I'm going to move to New Mexico with her."

Surprised at this last bit of information, Cope took her hand again. "Katie, you didn't tell me you were moving out of state." His tone was accusatory. The thought of his best female friend moving away, maybe forever, shocked him.

She squeezed his hand. "I'm sorry. I knew you'd be disappointed, and I didn't want to see that look on your face you just gave me."

"Wait a minute." Margaret's shocked voice interrupted. "You're not gay. Did this woman turn you? I can recommend a therapist."

To Katherine's credit, she gave a good-natured chuckle and smiled indulgently at Margaret. "I've always been attracted to women. It's not a mental illness. Didn't you ever wonder why Cope and I were such good friends all our lives and never dated?"

"I thought you just needed a push in the right direction."

"I'm in the right direction. So is Cope. He loves Dani, and I hope you can be happy for them."

"Yes, well, could be Bobby doesn't know this girl as well as he thinks he does."

"What's that supposed to mean?" Damn it, he was tired of his mother's attitude about his girlfriend. So what if she wasn't from a wealthy family? Who cares what her parents had done? This was about Dani. Sweet, gentle, vulnerable Dani.

"It means if you knew her better, you wouldn't be so quick to sleep with her. I hope you use protection when you're inside her." She spit the words at him. He'd never seen her so furious.

"Jesus, Mother. What a thing to say about the woman I love."

"There's something you should know about the woman you love. I didn't want to show you this, but it's time to tell you the truth." Margaret stepped back into the house and returned a few seconds later with her cell phone. She started a video and held the phone out so both Cope and Katherine could see it.

The sight of Dani in bed with Greg Henderson and another woman turned Cope's stomach. "Turn it off. Where did you get this? When was that taken?" It couldn't be recent. He refused to believe that this had happened while he and Dani were together.

"When she was dating Henderson. The private investigator I hired to check out your girlfriend dug it up. I didn't want to bring it to you, but since that girl"—Margaret wrinkled her nose on the word girl and continued—"refuses to stay away from you, it's time you realized what kind of whore you're dating."

"What do you mean she refuses to stay away from me? What have you done?" He'd been right all along. He should've trusted his feeling that something was wrong and confronted Dani.

Margaret looked panicked and took a backward step. "Nothing. I didn't do anything."

Cope didn't believe her. She'd always interfered, and he could tell she'd meddled now. *The video.* "You showed it to Dani?" Worse. "You threatened her with it."

"I was trying to help you, Bobby. She's trash. Her whole family is trash."

Big Cope stepped outside. "What's going on?" He looked from one to the other. "I heard raised voices."

Cope ignored him and grabbed Katherine by the hand. "Let's go. I have to talk to Dani. I can't be here anymore."

"Wait." Margaret's voice, commanding, stopped them, and they both turned and met her gaze. Cheeks puffed out, brows furrowed, Margaret resembled an angry chipmunk.

"What is it?" His voice came out tired, resigned. "What now?"

"If you insist on seeing her, you won't inherit anything. Tell him, Rupert."

"I'm sorry. Son, I have nothing against the girl, but we don't want someone like her burrowing into this family. We have to protect ourselves from gold diggers and pariahs."

"I can believe Mother would do this, but not you."

"Then you don't know me. It's not personal, son, it's business."

"Fuck you both. I don't care about your wealth. It's not business, Dad, it's personal." He turned on his heel and walked out, Katherine following him.

Cope drove Katherine home but decided it was too late to call Dani though it took him another twenty minutes to actually drop the idea. By the time he pulled out of Katherine's driveway, it was almost two o'clock. Dani was likely asleep and shooting always started early. He'd be one selfish S.O.B. if he called her now to talk about his needs, wants, and desires. Frustrated, he drove home, promising himself he'd call her first thing in the morning.

CHAPTER 33

Makeup and wardrobe ready, Dani prepared herself mentally for another day on the side of the mountain. The sun had barely cleared the horizon, and it looked perfect for filming. At least at this elevation, the heat and humidity weren't a problem.

Here, she was unable to receive phone calls from Cope. The cell service was sketchy, and they'd only be able to text. Calls went straight to voicemail. She'd noticed a message from him while she prepped, but couldn't retrieve it. She texted him to let him know she'd call him when she got home that night.

Though nervous at the prospect of talking to him, she ached to put her arms around him and feel his lips on hers. Surely, they could figure out a way to stay together. She left the trailer and waved to Ryan, who sat in a director's chair outside. Karen, an assistant, escorted Dani, and they walked to the clearing where the crew had set up the cameras.

Ferguson signaled he was ready, so Dani kicked off her ballerina flats and slipped on the high-heeled pumps her poor character was forced to wear. Today, she'd have to run in the damn things, too. In this scene, Felicity escapes from the cabin where she's being held and is chased through the forest to the edge of a cliff.

The stand-in would take over for the cliff scene, spending most of her time dangling over the gorge. Dani looked forward to the break she'd get during that time. She planned to nap in her trailer so she'd be able to stay awake when Cope came over later that night. The assistant director approached, holding out a roll of duct tape. Dani sighed and presented her wrists. At least they were binding her hands in front.

The shoot went well, and when the stand-in took over, Dani exchanged her heels with the ballerina flats for the return walk. "I'll be in my trailer, Jake."

When Ferguson didn't even glance up, she stepped toward him. The woman who'd escorted her from the trailer approached, and Dani grabbed her arm. "Karen, if Jake needs me, I'll be in my trailer."

"I'll walk you down."

Dani shook her head. "No, thanks. It's not far and my bodyguard is right there. Come and get me if I'm needed again. I'm tired and want to lie down for a bit."

"Yes, Miss Grayson."

One of the crew called to Karen, and she looked over, giving Dani the opportunity to scurry away. Every moment wasted cut into her precious naptime. She followed the dirt path back to the trailer.

No one was in sight. Why wasn't Ryan sitting outside? He was supposed to stay by her trailer during filming, since he wasn't part of the cast and crew. Everyone else was watching the shoot at the edge of the cliff.

"Ryan?" No response. Maybe he'd gone back to the car for something. No doubt he'd be back soon.

Inside the trailer, Dani went for her water. The glass bottle she used sat on the table, and she unscrewed the cap. Funny. She didn't remember leaving it sitting out. She liked her water cold and kept it in the fridge. She shrugged it off and took a long swallow. Even at room temperature, it was still refreshing.

Sweat streamed down her back and drenched her underarms. She'd take a shower before lying down, though that would mean doing the makeup and wardrobe routine over again. Too bad. They'd just have to deal with it. The dirt and dust coating her suit had worked its way inside, and she was itching as well as sweating.

She peeled off her clothes and turned on the water in the tiny stall at the back of the trailer. She'd have to be quick—the tank was small. The water trickled over her, and she washed her hair and body, frustrated at the low pressure. As she finished rinsing off, wooziness made her brace against the shower walls.

Dani turned off the water, stepped from the stall, and staggered toward the bed. Her knees buckled before she reached it. Her muscles weak, she fell onto her face. "Hel—" Couldn't speak. Vision blurred. Eyes closed. Darkness.

***

No service. Call you when I get home tonight.

It was the last message Cope received from Dani. He heard nothing from or about her until Katherine called him at work and told him to turn on the news. He switched on the TV hanging on the wall in his office and flipped to the news, icy fingers slow and clumsy.

The scene showed helicopters hovering around the mountain where Dani's film shoot was. A male voiceover spoke.

"John Madden, Miss Grayson's manager, arrived on the scene and has joined the search. Again, our top story, in progress, is the disappearance of Oscar-winning actress Daniella Grayson from the location of her current movie shoot for *Injury 2: Band-Aid Solution*. We'll have more for you as the story develops."

Cope muted the TV. "Jesus. How did this happen?" He had to get to the mountain. Where was the bodyguard? How could a famous actress disappear while filming a movie?

"I don't know. Want me to go with you? We can volunteer to help in the search."

"Hell yes. Right now."

"Okay. We'll get there, but I don't want you to kill yourself doing it. I'll change into hiking gear and pick you up. Should I meet you at your place?"

"No, come here. Just hurry."

Katherine promised to be there in thirty minutes and ended the call.

An hour-and-a-half later, they talked their way through a police checkpoint at the head of the trail leading up the mountain. Katherine drove up to the group of trailers that comprised the base camp for the location shoot. A staging area had been set up, and a woman and man stood beside a folding table and two chairs.

Katherine found a spot amongst the other cars and pulled over. She'd barely put the car into park when Cope flung open the door and jumped out. Katherine's door slammed as she got out on her side. His heart skipped a beat at the police tape around Dani's trailer. The couple near the table waved and greeted the new arrivals.

"Can we help you? I'm Andrew Holt," said the man, who looked to be in his mid-fifties. He waved at his companion, who wore a Los Angeles Police Department uniform. "This is PC Sophie Enders. You're Robert Copeland. I recognize you from the newspapers."

"That's right. Can you tell me what happened? Are you with the LAPD also? Where's Dani's bodyguard?"

PC Enders stepped forward. "Can I see some IDs?"

Cope frowned, frustrated, but he and Katherine both took out their wallets and handed over driver's licenses. When Enders acknowledged the identities, Cope said, "What happened?"

Holt held up a hand. "I'm not with the LAPD. I'm Danger Play security. The police believe Miss Grayson didn't leave of her own free will. There are signs she was abducted."

Cope's heart thundered in his chest and his mouth went dry. He turned to the police officer. "Who?"

"Greg Henderson might be involved. He hasn't been seen since last night. Miss Grayson arrived at this location early in the morning, prepared for the shoot, and did four hours of filming. She returned to her trailer at 11:00 AM and had a shower. It appears she collapsed getting out of the shower, and someone, likely Henderson, broke into her trailer and abducted her."

"No one saw this? Where's Ryan Pearlman? What the hell do I pay him for? He's supposed to be protecting her."

Holt and Enders exchanged glances, sending a shiver of fear through Cope at their expressions. "What is it? Where's Ryan?"

Enders replied. "He's in the hospital. We found him behind Miss Grayson's trailer. He's been shot, but he'll survive."

"Jesus Christ. What's Henderson doing?"

Another exchange of glances. Enders again broke the silence. "Sit, Mr. Copeland."

"No. What aren't you telling me? More than half the day is gone. Where'd he take her?"

Enders reached out and touched Cope's shoulder, stroked his arm, a gesture meant to reassure, but instead it heightened the fear. Cope stepped back, gritting his teeth, face grimacing in pain.

"Where are you looking? Is she out on the mountain somewhere?" It came out an airy whisper, almost a wheeze. *Oh, God. Dani.* His heart hurt. What if he lost her? His arms longed to hold her. If he could see her again, he'd take her in his arms and cover her with kisses. *Please, God, just let me see her again.*

"Tell me. I have a right to know. She's my fiancée." A lie, but a temporary white lie. He'd rectify it as soon as they were together again.

"We're doing everything we can to find her. He took her away in his vehicle, but has since abandoned it. We don't know what he's driving now. The car was ditched in Culver City."

"Will he harm her?" Cope couldn't bring himself to ask if Henderson intended to kill her. If anything happened to her, he wouldn't be able to live with himself. He should have had two bodyguards watching her. He should have—Katherine interrupted his desperate musings.

"Pull yourself together. We'll find her."

"Sit, Mr. Copeland." Enders used a grip on his arm to guide him to a chair. "I'd like to ask you some questions."

He let her press him into the seat and waited for her to say something.

"When was the last time you communicated with Miss Grayson?"

"This morning." Cope showed her the text Dani had sent him. "We get no chance to talk on the phone when she's up here, so we kept in touch this way."

"Has Miss Grayson said anything to you about Greg Henderson? Had he tried to contact her since he was released on bail?"

"If he had, she wasn't telling me. Have you checked her phone records?"

"That's in process. I was hoping you had additional information."

Cope shook his head. That snake probably kept to himself so her guard would be down. How to find her? He had to think. If the cops let him join the search, they'd steer him to the least likely place. They wouldn't want him to be the one to find Henderson. He'd have to slip off by himself if he had any hope of finding Dani soon.

"Answer the question," Cope insisted. "Do you think he'll harm her?"

"He might if anyone tries to take her from him. Henderson has at least one gun with him."

"Did he stay around here?"

"We've gone over this place with dogs, and there's no reason to believe he's on the mountain. We're using Culver City as the starting point for the search, though we don't know what kind of car we're looking for. There's been no report of a vehicle stolen in that area, so we're speculating that he had one waiting. Video surveillance might have picked that up, and if it did, we'll put out an APB."

"Have you searched his house?"

"We have officers there right now. If they find anything, they'll alert us. There's nothing to do now but wait."

Restless and frustrated, Cope stood and made his way to the trailer. "Can I go in?"

"Yes, if Danger Play permits it. The police have already searched it and collected whatever was there."

"Go ahead, Mr. Copeland," Bennett said.

Cope strode to the trailer, yanked the tape off the door, and stepped inside.

CHAPTER 34

Groggy and nauseated, Dani regained consciousness dangling from the shoulder of whoever had her in the fireman's carry. A heavy-looking backpack bumped against her head with every step. She groaned. The man—she knew it was a man by the muscles and the sweaty male scent—stopped and set her on her ass among the leaves.

Before she could see who was there, Dani rolled onto her hands and knees and vomited. The odor of bile assaulted her, and she retched again. And again. And again. Whatever was in her stomach wanted out so bad it hurt. Sobs cheered on the vomiting, and she wished she could pass out again.

When the cramps and spasms eased, she crawled backward away from the puddle of puke. A hand holding a bottle of water, cap off, appeared under her nose, and she accepted it, grateful.

"Thanks." Manners first, then relief. Dani chugged.

"Not so fast. You'll be sick again."

A chill shot up her spine, and the blood whooshed out of her face. *Greg Henderson.* Her head snapped up to look at him, and oh, God, it was Henderson looming over her. The bottle dropped from her fingers, and she backed away, scuttling crab-like on hands and feet. Weak and dehydrated, she collapsed in the dirt.

He caught up to her and slid his hands under her armpits.

Dani struggled, but it was no use, and she gave a frustrated sob. "What have you done?" Grief and rage saturated her words, but they came out clear enough.

"I came back for you, babe. No one can keep us apart." He dropped to the ground and pulled her into his lap, arms viselike around her torso.

Memory fuzzy, she tried to recollect what had happened. She'd been filming. The scene had ended, and the next one involved the stunt double and two other actors. She must have returned to the trailer, but she couldn't remember doing it. She checked out her clothes. She wore a T-shirt, jeans, and sneakers, but had no memory of putting them on.

"Have you lost your mind? You're out on bail."

"I can't live without you, baby. We belong together. We're perfect together."

"No, we're not. Let me go before you get in more trouble. When Jake finds out I'm gone, he'll look for me. Please. Take me back. This is crazy."

His arm snaked away from her body. He gripped her hair, and yanked her head back.

Dani cried out, more from shock than pain.

"Shut up. Dumb bitch. Keep that mouth shut. I'll tell you when you can speak, and then you keep your tone respectful. Got that?"

She nodded. Henderson was crazy. He had to be. She flashed back to when he'd attacked her in her apartment and shuddered.

"That's right. You're my little doll. My girl." The hand released her hair and stroked her cheek. He was gentle now, but that could change in an instant. She'd seen this Jekyll and Hyde routine when they'd dated, though it hadn't been frequent, and it hadn't seemed so deadly. It had scared her even then.

Afraid he'd hit her, but desperate to find out his intentions, she leaned into him as though resting against him the way she used to when they were dating.

When his breathing slowed, his chest rising and falling against her back, she whispered his name. "Greg?"

He stirred, one arm tightening around her body. His mouth nuzzled her hair. "My love?" His breath blew on her, and she smelled a trace of alcohol.

So he'd concocted this stupid stunt after a night of drinking? Dani wondered when he'd had his last drink. Maybe when he sobered up, he'd come to his senses and take her back.

Henderson's hand continued to stroke her cheek, her hair. He laid a gentle kiss on her temple.

Ask him. Ask him now, or you'll be too terrified to ever say anything. "Where are we going?" She'd excised the fear from her voice, making it low and gentle.

"Our place. No one will ever find us there," he said quietly, not edged with hysteria or anger. The tone was good, but Dani's terror skyrocketed at the words.

She looked around for the first time since she'd awoken and saw they sat on a dirt trail covered in oak leaves, fir needles, and other natural debris. Evergreen trees and big old oak trees stretched away from the path on either side. The trail led up.

Were they still in the mountains near the shoot? She hoped so. If she escaped, help might be easy to find, especially if the police were already looking for her.

"Can you walk?" Again gentle. Courteous. A light kiss on the cheek, two lovers nestled together, resting before resuming their journey.

"Yes." A little too loud, too fearful. Tears welled up in her eyes, and she squeezed them shut. The salty water ran down her face, and, afraid he'd get upset if he knew she was crying, she pressed her hands to her cheeks, obliterating the wet streaks. She took a deep breath and exhaled, forcing herself to stay calm. She wasn't tied up, which worked in her favor. She'd cooperate, and when he let his guard down, she'd find a way out.

Henderson released her, stood, and held his hand out. Dani grasped it and let him pull her up. When his arm slid around her waist, she forced herself to reciprocate and lean on him, and he led her up the trail.

***

A picture of Dani and Cope lay in its frame on the floor under shattered glass. Cope recalled the afternoon she'd taken it—that perfect picnic on the beach when their future looked as bright as the white sand reflecting the setting sun. A selfie, snapped while they canoodled on a blanket after a walk along the beach. The sight of it amped up the worry, the heartache, the fear, and brought the threat of tears with it. Cope gritted his teeth and snatched the picture off the floor.

How like her to have had it printed and framed. He picked the glass out of it and set the picture on the table, the sight of the happy couple in the photo tugging at his heart. A wet spot in front of the shower stall caught his eye, and he crouched before it, running his hands over the dampness.

Cope pictured her stepping from the shower. Something made her fall, but, thankfully, there were no blood stains. He scanned the room. Nothing out of place aside from the wet carpet and the broken picture frame. If there had been anything useful, the police would've taken it. Cope picked up the framed photo and left the trailer.

When he stepped outside, he noticed how long the shadows were. The air was getting cooler. He hoped to God Dani was okay, and they'd find her soon.

He turned to Holt and Enders. "What's your next move? Seems they're gone and won't come back here."

"Agreed," Enders replied. "I'm pulling out soon." She eyed Cope for a moment, then said, "Don't do anything foolish, Mr. Copeland. We'll find her. If you think of something that might help with the search, call me." She gave him her card.

Katherine moved to Cope's side and put her arm around him. "Let's go. I'll take you home."

He didn't reply, but as soon as they pulled away from the lot, he said,

"Drive to Henderson's apartment."

He heard her sudden intake of breath. "We can't do that."

"Then take me home to get my car. If you don't want to come with me, I'll go by myself."

Reluctantly, she agreed to go along, but when they arrived at the apartment, a crowd of reporters surrounded the place, and Cope told her to keep driving.

"I've got an idea. Drive to Ben's." He should have thought of his brother sooner. With his help, they could have Dani home and Henderson behind bars by morning.

***

By the time Dani and Henderson reached the cabin that was their destination, he was carrying her. As the sun dipped behind the trees, he set her on a Muskoka chair and fished in his bag for a key.

The oaks were sparser here, the pine trees taking over. Dani's head throbbed, and she thought she might pass out again. A long hike without food compounded whatever he'd drugged her with.

The door swung open. He hauled her out of the seat. When she collapsed against him, he lifted her into his arms.

"I'll carry you across the threshold, babe. Our new home." He kissed her nose, and she didn't have the strength to protest.

Her eyelids slid closed.

When Dani opened her eyes again, she realized she'd slept. The headache had disappeared, and she lay in a bed, a thick, fluffy comforter covering her. Bound hand and foot with duct tape, she was naked.

Twilight filtered through a window in the opposite wall. How long had she been out? Where was Henderson? She listened to the silence. Maybe he'd gone out or had fallen asleep. If so, she should try to escape before he returned.

Dani struggled the comforter off and sat, spinning her feet onto the floor. After a deep breath in, she stood. Thankfully, Henderson was an idiot and had forgotten she'd been trained to escape from duct tape when they'd filmed their first movie together. She raised her arms above her head and smashed them on her belly. The tape split apart, and she ripped it off her wrists. Then she crouched and peeled it off her ankles.

She scanned the room for her clothes. Nothing. There was a closet, but when she checked it, she found it locked. He wasn't a complete idiot then. She tiptoed to the window and peered out. It was getting dark. If she climbed out the window and escaped, she'd be naked and in danger of being found by predators before anyone rescued her. Henderson probably counted on her realizing that. What he didn't understand was how

151

desperately she wanted to get away from him.

Dani unlocked the window and raised the lower sash. As she gripped the screen to lift it out, she heard a sound behind her. A whimper escaped her lips, and she turned to face Henderson.

"What do you think you're doing?"

"I was getting air. I needed air." Her voice shook, and she folded her arms over her breasts, attempting to cover her nakedness.

"Do you think I'm a fucking idiot?"

Yes. "No. I didn't know where I was. I wanted to look outside and get some air."

Face turning red, he pounced on her. The first blow knocked Dani to the floor, and then he straddled her as she lay on her back. He grasped her wrists in one hand and held them above her head.

"Greg, no. Please. Don't." Her jaw ached where he'd hit her. She'd have a fat lip from that.

"I'm afraid you need to learn discipline, babe. What did I tell you about respect? Speak to me with respect." He spit out the P sound when he said "respect," and in a moment of lunacy, she almost screamed "say it; don't spray it."

Henderson hit her on the side of the face, open palm. Again. Again. She lost count by the time he stopped, and her ears rang. The only sound was the smack of skin on skin and Dani's hitched, ragged breathing. She refused to scream or beg or cry.

"I don't want to hit you, but you're making me do it. You wanted to climb out the window. Don't lie. Tell me that's what you wanted to do, and I'll forgive you. Just tell me the truth."

Oh, God. Was this a trick? She tested it. "I told you the truth. Where would I go? I'm naked. There could be mountain lions out there."

"Liar!" He stood, grabbed her by the hair, and dragged her to the bed. This time she did scream, she did beg, and she most definitely cried. "Greg, please. No. You're right. I was scared. I wanted to climb out. Please. I'm sorry."

He threw her on the bed, and Dani frantically burrowed into the quilt, wanting to hide. He put a hand on her throat and squeezed, then released. "Don't fucking move. Do you understand?"

"Yes."

He stomped from the room, and Dani huddled on the bed, too terrified to do anything else. Suddenly, she flashed back to when she was four years old. Home alone with her mother, Dani had spilled a glass of milk on the living room carpet. Lilli backhanded her, then grabbed her by the hair, shoved her nose in the mess, and dragged her into the bedroom. She ordered the little girl to wait on the bed and left the room. Dani heard her cleaning the milk, understanding that the real punishment would begin when Lilli returned.

Henderson burst back into the room, snapping Dani back to the present, and she screamed, her screams echoing through the cabin. He carried the duct tape, scissors, and a belt.

"Shut up, you stupid bitch, or I'll give you a reason to scream."

Dani cut off the screams. She'd learned long ago that it was best to obey without hesitation.

"Lie on your stomach."

"Greg, please. Please." Dani didn't know what else to say. Surely, he understood what she begged for.

"Now, baby, I have to teach you a lesson." He sounded regretful. *This will hurt me more than it'll hurt you* hung in the air between them. "Lie down. Don't make me ask you again, or I'll have to punish you for that, too."

Dani lay on her stomach, body shaking with cold, fear, and ceaseless sobs. The sound of the duct tape peeling off the roll brought her close to screaming and begging again, but she stifled it. With gentle hands, he bound her wrists above her head and then taped her ankles.

"So sorry, baby. This'll hurt, but you brought it on yourself. You'll get five lashes, and I want you to count them with me. Understand?"

"Yes." Choking. She needed air and gulped like a landed fish.

Henderson raised the belt.

CHAPTER 35

Cope sat waiting on a chair in Ben's office. Katherine stood next to Ben and watched what he did. Cope tried to stifle the impatience that made him so restless he'd spent most of the last two hours pacing. Should hacking into someone's files take this long?

Ben had tried to explain what he was doing when he got fed up with his younger brother's nervous energy, but it was jabber to Cope. When Ben got technical, it made Cope think accessing Henderson's email and other files would be impossible. After that, they were still searching for something they'd recognize only when they found it.

"I have it." Ben waved to Cope, who jumped from his chair to peer at the monitor.

An email message displayed on the screen, and Ben toggled to another window. "Here. See that map? It leads to a cabin Henderson bought two years ago under another name."

"Let's go. We have to get to her before he hurts her." *Or kills her.* That threat was real. Too many times women ended up murdered by exes who refused to let them go.

Katherine moved toward the door, and Cope stopped her. "No. Too dangerous."

"You're not leaving me behind." She confronted him, fists on hips, feet planted on the floor.

Cope pulled Enders's card out of his wallet and handed it to Katherine. "Call the cops. Tell them where we think he is, but give us a half-hour lead. I don't want Dani killed in a shootout."

She hesitated.

"Please. I need you safe and the cops on the way."

Resignation showed on her face and she took the card. "Okay. Go get your girlfriend. Be careful."

He leaned in, kissed her cheek, and gave her a quick hug. "Okay, Ben. Let's go."

Ben retrieved a Colt .45 from his desk. "Ready, bro. Just gotta grab my ammo."

***

Punishment over, Henderson cut the duct tape from Dani's wrists and ankles and helped her climb under the comforter. To her horror, he stripped off his clothes and climbed into bed with her.

She recoiled.

"No, babe. None of that. You're mine now. Just us, together forever." He put his arms around her and yanked her to him.

Afraid of another whipping, she put her head on his shoulder and pretended it was Cope she leaned against. Eyes closed, she pictured herself back in Cope's arms. She was thirsty and wondered if she'd be risking another beating asking for water. Her mouth was so dry. Chills wracked her body, and she shivered.

"Are you okay, baby? Do you need anything?" The concern in his voice made anger swell inside her, but she suppressed it.

As she had with her mother, she'd have to play pretend. Pretend everything was normal. Pretend it was okay. Don't cry. Don't complain. Most of all, be invisible, silent. Speak when spoken to. She'd been spoken to now, so she replied. "Water, please."

Henderson leaned over and kissed her cheek and her lips.

Dani flinched, but he didn't notice—she'd have to do better next time, make it appear she was okay with it without encouraging more.

He got out of bed, said "Don't move," and walked out.

Dani took him literally and remained frozen until he returned. He came back with two bottles of water and gave one to her. Should she thank him? Or would that be speaking without permission? If she didn't thank him, he might get angry at her rudeness. If she did, he might get angry that she spoke. One way to find out: "Thank you."

She sipped the water while he slipped back under the covers. Her heart beat rapidly, sweat broke out under her arms, and her spine prickled at the thought of what would happen next.

"Had enough water?"

It was a question anyone might ask, and under normal circumstances, it would be considered polite. Coming from Henderson right now, it chilled Dani to the bone. She tipped the bottle to her lips again, sipping, buying time—even another second helped.

When she took yet another slow sip, he realized what she was doing and grabbed the bottle from her. He recapped it and set it on the nightstand next to the bed. "It's been a long time, babe. Come here. I've dreamed about fucking you ever since we did it on set."

"Greg, please." Dani wriggled to the edge of the bed, but didn't get out.

His expression grew dark, the frown vicious. "Behave, Daniella. I've been wanting this. You know you want it, too. I don't want any trouble from you."

"I'm not feeling well." Maybe she could talk him out of it. At least keep him talking though she'd have to choose her words with extreme care. "I haven't eaten since—I don't even know how long. Please. Can we eat first?" She kept her voice even. No whining. Normal speaking voice. Reasonable.

"Okay." He got out of bed again, unlocked and opened the closet, and took out a woman's bathrobe, which he tossed on the bed. "Put that on and come with me."

Dani moved slowly and deliberately. *Normal.* It became her mantra. She picked up the robe and slipped into it, grateful to conceal her body. Henderson retrieved a robe for himself, put it on, and took her hand. He guided her out of the bedroom and into the main living area of the cabin.

Had she been here with Cope, she'd have called it quaint, even lovely. The furniture was rustic, and a large, fieldstone fireplace dominated the living room. An open kitchen had all the conveniences: fridge, stove, dishwasher—even an apartment-sized stacked washer and dryer. A pine table with seating for eight people was the focal point in the dining area.

Henderson motioned for her to sit at the table, so she pulled out the closest chair and sat down. The silence got to her, but she was afraid to break it, and looked around instead, trying to find a potential weapon. It hadn't escaped her he'd had a woman's robe on hand. Had he been planning this, or did the robe belong to a former girlfriend?

Dani peeked into the fridge when he opened it and noted it was stuffed with fresh food. He pulled out a prepared salad and a bottle of dressing and set them on the table. An urge to help overcame her, and she almost stood when she remembered he'd told her to sit. She folded her hands on the table in front of her and realized she was chewing on the inside of her cheek. It was a nervous habit she hadn't indulged in since she'd lived with her mother.

He opened a pantry, and Dani scoped that out as well: lots of canned goods, cereals, pastas, and rice. The door slammed shut before she saw more, and Henderson held a French loaf in his hand. He returned to the fridge and took out various cheeses. By the time he finished, he'd amassed a decent meal.

"What would you like to drink? Wine?" He held up a bottle of Sauvignon blanc and tilted it toward the glass he'd set by her plate.

A direct question. Answer him. "No, just water, please. I left it in the bedroom. May I go get it?" Best to ask. If she asked, she was being respectful, and if she was being respectful, he wouldn't get angry.

"I'll get it. Don't move." He strode into the bedroom, his pace hurried. So he didn't trust her at all. How long would it take to lull him into a false contentment? She feared it would be too long.

Oh, God, she didn't want to sleep with him, and if he realized that, he'd hurt her. She had to get out of here. She caught herself before she folded onto the table in despair. *No, don't let him see fear, or he'll suspect I'm planning escape.*

He returned and set her water on the table next to her hands, which rested, still clasped, on the table in front of her plate. As he walked past her, he stroked her hair and then her cheek. Her mouth dry, Dani swallowed, and when he sat next to her, she picked up the water and drank.

"Is this okay? Need anything else?" So polite, he was. So solicitous.

Shrieks welled up inside her, and it took everything she had not to open her mouth and scream until she woke from this nightmare. "Fine, thanks."

He poured himself wine, and Dani's stomach lurched. It was worse when he drank. When they'd dated, they'd both drank to excess. When Dani drank too much, she became livelier, then wound down, passed out, and, if she'd really overdone it, she'd puke. But when Henderson drank too much, he became quieter, then meaner, to the point where he'd frighten her.

He picked up the knife and cut slices of cheese, and, when he was done, set down the knife out of her reach. Every move he made, her gaze followed. If he touched something, she considered its use as a weapon.

At least she was no longer naked. With food in her stomach, she might muster up the strength to attempt escape, though not if she had to fight her way out. But if she tried to slip out after he was asleep, she'd have to have sex with him first.

Panic rose in her again, and she distracted herself by nibbling on the food and sipping her water. He'd given her a fork for the salad, but she knew she'd never be able to stab him with it. Sure, she could work herself up to hate him enough to do it, but she'd never incapacitate him, and a wounded, angry Henderson might kill her. He was capable of murder, she was sure of it.

"Tomorrow, I'll show you the view in the back. There's a mountain stream where we can fish. It's gorgeous." He smiled at her, a big, smarmy, motherfucking grin like they were lovers on a romantic getaway.

Her hand tightened on the fork. "Sounds lovely."

He hadn't asked a question but was making conversation. Amendment to the rule: *speak when he seems to want to converse even if he hasn't asked a direct question.*

Sweat beaded on the back of Dani's neck, and she rubbed it with a napkin. Another sip of water calmed her nerves. She'd lost her appetite, but forced herself to eat. If she escaped, she'd need her strength.

All too soon, her salad bowl was empty, and she couldn't stomach anything else.

He noticed and stopped eating. "Had enough?"

Dani gulped water, saw that almost three-quarters of the bottle of wine was gone, and sought the courage to answer. "Yes." A whisper. No good. He'd pick up on the fear. She cleared her throat. "Yes. Thank you." Clearer. Better.

"Shall we retire to the bedroom, my love?"

"We shouldn't leave this stuff out. Let me help you clean it up first." No shaking in her voice. She was giving the performance of her life—for her life.

"Yes. You're right. Sit. I'll take care of everything. Don't move."

Dani held her breath while he wrapped up the food, rinsed the dishes, and put everything away. It didn't take as long as she would've liked, and all too soon, he was done and heading toward her. Her gaze darted around the room, but she saw no way out, nothing she could use as a weapon. Unable to help it, she begged.

"Please, don't make me sleep with you. Not tonight."

He grabbed her by the arms, eyes sparking anger. "You belong to me now, and you do as I tell you."

"I don't belong to you. I don't belong to anyone. Let me go. Please. You must know what you're doing is wrong. Why did you do this?"

In answer, he kissed her on the mouth, hard, forcing her to feel his desire. She tried to pull away and failed. He pressed his body against her, pressed his hardness against her.

Henderson lifted his mouth from hers and with one hand, shoved her head forward so she saw his penis thrusting out of the part in his robe. "See what you caused? Tease. You tease me and then you don't want to give me the relief I need. You have an obligation."

He lifted her in his arms and carried her into the bedroom, her sobs now the only sound she could hear.

CHAPTER 36

Cope and Ben had to leave their car at the bottom of a trail that led to the cabin where they suspected Dani might be held. They spotted a car amongst the trees and recognized it as a vehicle the police had described when the APB went out on Henderson.

Ben had his gun ready, and Cope led the way. He hurried though the dark trail was littered with rocks and tree roots that tripped them up despite the flashlight he carried. When the cabin came into view, Cope motioned for Ben to watch the front of the house while he went around back.

Everything was dark inside. Cope tried to look in a window, but it was shielded by a curtain. He approached the side of the house and found an uncovered kitchen window. He'd have to hurry. The cops would be close behind them. By the time the police arrived, he wanted to have Henderson gift wrapped for them.

Silence blanketed the house and surrounding yard. Mouth drawing into a tight, grim line, Cope shoved aside thoughts of what Dani might have suffered in the time she was missing. If he didn't, he'd kill Henderson on sight. The kitchen window was open, the screen the only obstacle. Cope removed the screen, raised the sash higher, and climbed in.

Once inside, he sat for a moment on the kitchen counter, letting his eyes adjust to the semi-dark room. A faint glow from the LCD on the stove and moonlight shining in through the windows afforded the only illumination. The front door should be on his right. He eased to the floor.

The boards creaked under him as he walked, and he froze. Breath held, he waited and listened. Nothing. One foot forward. Another step. By the time he reached the front door, sweat drenched him.

He ran his hands along the door where the faint outline of the doorknob was visible. Over it was the deadbolt. He quietly opened the door, left it propped open, and returned to the kitchen without waiting to see where Ben was. His priority was getting to Dani.

The kitchen and dining area abutted a living room on the right. A sliding door beside the fireplace in the living room lead to the porch. Cope crossed the kitchen into the hallway beyond and followed it, opening doors as he went. The first one led to the bathroom, the next, a closet. A noise behind him told him Ben had entered the house. Not caring about silence anymore, Cope picked up the pace.

He opened the bedroom door. It was darker than the rest of the house, shades blacking out the windows. The king bed was occupied, but Cope couldn't tell who was in it. At first it looked like one large person. He drew closer, and in the dim light from the clock radio, he saw Henderson spooned around Dani. Cope screamed in rage, grabbed Henderson by the arm, and yanked him to the ground. As soon as he hit the floor, he moaned and puked.

Cope leaped out of the way, and, leaving the kidnapper to writhe on the floor in his own vomit, rushed to Dani. Cope's heart broke at the sight of her bound hand and foot, hands secured behind her back with duct tape, her pale skin mottled with bruises. Rage bubbled up in him and it took all his self-control not to round on Henderson and kill him. Before Cope could flick on his flashlight, the overhead light went on. Ben had arrived.

"Make sure that bastard on the floor doesn't move, Ben."

"Got him."

Oh, God, Dani. Cope couldn't speak. Since she had her back to him, he could see welts covered her back, butt, and thighs. Her arms were bruised and her fingers swollen. He grabbed the scissors off the night table and cut through the tape on her wrists and ankles. As he peeled the remaining tape from her skin, he noted drug paraphernalia and traces of white powder next to the lamp. Henderson had been doing drugs. What if he'd forced them on Dani, too?

Where were the cops? Now Cope wished he hadn't told Katherine to wait thirty minutes. Henderson would be too out of it to resist arrest—he wasn't even sober enough to make it to the toilet to puke. Groans from the floor indicated Henderson was conscious and still struggling with nausea.

Cope pulled Dani into his arms. His gut lurched when she remained limp and unresponsive though she was breathing. Her blackened eyes stayed closed, and her head flopped against his chest. "Call nine-one-one and get an ambulance here," Cope called out to Ben.

He pulled the comforter over her naked body and held her. When he checked her pulse, it seemed normal.

"Dani." He bent his head to hers and kissed her hair. "Baby, please wake up. I'm here. You'll be okay now."

She was still unconscious when the police and paramedics arrived.

***

Dani had a concussion, and the doctors told Cope they didn't know when she might wake up. She'd slipped into a coma while Henderson had slept. He'd tried to rape her, failed to get it up, probably from the alcohol and coke he'd consumed, and then beat her in a fit of rage. He claimed he couldn't remember doing any of that. At last, he was in jail with no chance of bail, but now the waiting game was on as Cope sat by Dani's bedside and held her hand.

Liz, John Madden, people from Star Power and Danger Play, and others who cared for Dani stopped by. Many more sent flowers. A shrine grew in front of Dani's apartment building, and fans held candlelight vigils.

Reporters had tried to get into her room, but the hospital staff kept them at bay. Cope had hired a bodyguard to stand outside her door, which kept out even the most clever and determined gossip hunters.

Red-rimmed eyes betrayed Cope had shed tears, but now that he was cried out, he sat staring at her dry-eyed. Dani's poor, bruised face was calm, her chest rising and falling in a slow rhythm as though she slept in peace.

He hoped that was true, but he also hoped that when he talked, she heard him wherever her mind wandered. And he did talk because so much had been left unsaid before she'd disappeared, and what if this was his only chance to say it?

"I found out what my mother did. That's why you were so distant, why you avoided me. What a struggle that must have been. So sorry you felt as though you weren't good enough for my family. I love you, Daniella. I'll always love you. When you get better, I'll spend the rest of my life showing you how much."

Someone cleared her throat, and Cope turned to see who had walked in despite the bodyguard outside. His mother stood in the open doorway, a vase of flowers in her hands. "May I come in?"

Lost for words, Cope nodded. The strength to fight with Margaret had disappeared. All he felt was sadness at how her greed and narcissism had torn them apart.

"I wanted to deliver these myself and see you." Margaret drew closer to Dani's bed and held the flowers out to Cope.

He rose and took the elaborate arrangement from her, setting it on the floor.

She waved her arms at the other bouquets and potted plants that covered every available surface. "She's popular."

Cope nodded again, still unable to speak.

"I'm sorry, Bobby. Will she get better?"

"I don't know." His voice broke when he said it. "They don't know why she's unconscious. Everything seems fine with her brain, but she won't wake up."

"I overheard what you said to her. I didn't mean to eavesdrop."

He shrugged. "It's not important."

"Yes, it is. I've been so awful."

Cope returned to his seat next to Dani's bed and clasped her hand in his. "You won't get an argument from me."

"Ben told me what happened—how you two rescued her. That maniac could've killed you. Or Ben."

Cope stared at her, narrowing his eyes, frowning. "If we hadn't gone, she might've died in her sleep. Henderson was too messed up to notice he'd beaten her into a coma. She'd be another statistic. Another woman killed by her sadistic-as-fuck ex."

"If something had happened to you, I wouldn't be able to forgive myself. I couldn't go on if I'd lost you or Ben. My life would've been ruined."

"You? Why is this about you?" He honestly didn't know whether to laugh or cry. At least she was here trying to do something positive. Possibly. An apology usually meant something good, though with Margaret, you could never be certain.

"My God, Bobby. Let me say sorry for what I've done. I drove you away, maybe forever, and I didn't think it important at the time. It was more important to force you to see things my way or have you suffer for it until you did."

"Your way is cruel and judgmental. That's not me."

"I wanted to keep you from getting hurt."

He brushed imaginary hair from Dani's face and placed a hand on her cheek. She felt warm—not feverish—just warm, and her skin was soft and smooth. He was certain the swelling on her face had diminished.

When she was awake, and the swelling was gone, he promised himself he'd kiss her often. He turned to look at Margaret again. "You hurt her. Because of you, she avoided me, and Henderson got to her." He shook his head. "No. I'm sorry. That's not true. I refuse to play your game and lay blame where it's undeserved. Henderson got to her at work despite the bodyguard."

"How is the bodyguard?"

"Home from the hospital, but he can't return to work for another month at least. He almost died."

"I'm sorry."

"Me too. Ryan blames himself." Cope chuckled, but it was without warmth or mirth. "He blames himself; I blame myself. We make a wonderful pair."

"It's not your fault, darling."

He winced. *Darling.* Whenever she used it, the superficiality of it struck

162

him like a slap.

"Bobby, I'm sorry, and I hope Dani recovers. When she does, please bring her to the house. I'd like to apologize in person and hope she'll forgive me."

Startled, he looked in her eyes, but all he saw was worry. "She will. Dani's kind like that. What changed your mind?"

"I've been following the story on the news. You're quite a hero. If you love her that should be enough for me. I can't say I'm happy with your choice, but I won't fight it anymore."

"What else, Mother? You didn't just have a sudden epiphany." He knew her too well. She was his mother, and he loved her despite her faults and out of obligation. But she strong-armed his father, which angered Cope. Then he realized what else was behind this. "What happened between Dad and Nate?"

Cope had always suspected she'd had something to do with the parting of ways between Nate and Big Cope. Margaret opened her mouth to speak, but he cut her off as he figured it out. "Jesus. The woman he married. You didn't approve of her, and when you forced him to choose between his friendship with Dad and the woman he loved …" Cope shook his head. "How did you expect it to turn out? You can't give someone an ultimatum like that."

"That woman was a gold digger. They divorced three years into the marriage, and she took Nate for half of everything he'd worked so hard to make. I was right."

"That's why you should've stuck by him. He needed your support, and instead of being there for him, you cut him out of your lives. How can Dad let you do that to people he loves?" Cope paused, held up his hand, forestalling her again. "Dad loves you that much. I hope you're happy."

"No, I'm not—not for a long time, and I don't want this anymore." She went to the bed and looked at Dani. "Whatever her past, she didn't deserve what happened. I hope she gets better soon."

"Thanks for coming."

She smiled. "Forgive me?"

"Of course."

A loud sigh crossed her lips, and she shook her head. "It'll be a day of penance for me. I'm visiting Nate now. If I'm lucky, he'll be as forgiving as you are. Your father has missed him, and I was wrong to force them apart."

Cope stood again and hugged her. When she left, he sat on the edge of Dani's bed and took her hand. "Did you hear that, my beauty? Things are getting better. Please, come back to me."

CHAPTER 37

Dani holds her father's hand, reluctant to release it. Their time together has been so precious, and now he says she has to leave.

"But I just got here." It comes out a wail. This place has been a comfortable haven, and she wants to stay.

"We'll be together again, I promise. But it's not your time."

"Just a little longer, Daddy. I don't want to leave you."

"It'll be okay. You have to go, but I'll be with you. I've always been nearby, pumpkin."

Dani smiles at his use of the childhood endearment. "I love you so much, Daddy."

Paul Grayson hugs his daughter and kisses her cheeks. "I love you, too. Remember, I'm not really gone."

"Daddy, wait."

Another voice, not her father's, cut through the disappointment and longing. She'd heard it sometimes even while she was with her dad. The voice, familiar, reassuring, guided her to wakefulness, and excitement and relief surged through her when she recognized Cope.

He was reading.

Dani listened for a moment, not wanting to interrupt him, until she realized she didn't know where she was, and the last thing she remembered was … *Oh, God. Greg.* She opened her eyes.

Gaze absorbed in the book, a novel, Cope didn't notice Dani's eyes were open and continued to read aloud. "Carolyn found herself crying again and swiped the tears off her face. The prospect of morning and what that would bring scared her—"

"Cope?"

The book fell to the floor when he leaped up and buzzed the nurse. "Dani. Thank God. How do you feel?"

"Hungry. Sore. What happened? How did I get here? Where's Greg?"

Cope took her hand and leaned close, examining her face. "I'll tell you everything, but wait until after the nurse gets here and checks you out."

She yawned and stretched as the nurse entered the room, smiling. "Welcome back, Miss Grayson. How are you feeling?"

"Like I could eat my arm."

"I'll get the doctor and then find you some food," she said and checked Dani's vitals.

When the nurse left, Cope perched on the edge of the bed and leaned in to kiss her lips. "I've been wanting to give those lips a proper kiss for days."

"I'm so glad to see you, Robert."

He smiled and kissed her again. "God, I was so afraid I'd lose you."

"You came for me."

"Of course. I couldn't leave you. He almost killed you."

"How did you find me?"

Cope told her how they'd cracked into Henderson's accounts and found the cabin. "It was a long shot, but it made sense he'd take you somewhere off the radar. Henderson had bought the place under another name. I don't know how—something for the courts to figure out, I guess. When we arrived, he was so out of it, I walked in and took you away. He's locked up now and won't bother you again."

Tears welled up in her eyes. "Robert, before all this happened, I avoided you. While I was with Greg, I promised myself that if I saw you again, I'd tell you the truth. I never wanted to hurt you. It tore me apart to be away from you. I'm so sorry."

"It's okay. I understand what happened. My mother and I talked."

"Margaret, she—"

"Shh. It's okay. Everything's okay. We'll be all right now. You're back."

***

The car left the highway, and when Dani realized where they headed, she smiled and glanced at Cope.

He grinned back at her. "I wanted to take you someplace special for your first full day back on your feet. Since you return to work tomorrow and spent the last two weeks cooped up, today will be outside and all about you."

"Thank you. Beautiful day for it, too. No clouds and plenty of sunshine."

When they reached the spot overlooking the ocean where Cope parked the car, Dani was surprised to see other cars. She frowned. Had other people discovered their secret spot? She hoped it wasn't reporters. Wasn't this private property?

Cope said nothing, but parked the car and helped her out. He guided her to the trail.

She stopped walking. "What about the basket? I thought we were coming here for a picnic?"

He arched his brows, gave her a sly smile, and then scooped her up and carried her down the path.

Half delighted and half fearing he'd drop her, Dani threw her arms around his neck and buried her face in his shoulder, giggling. As he set her back on her feet, she heard a smattering of applause. She looked up to find everyone she knew gathered together on the sand. Patio tables, each with its own umbrella. Flowers. Lights, accenting the place settings clustered around a pedestal fire pit. The beach had been set up for a celebration.

Her gaze met Liz's, then went to John, who was with his wife and kids. The executives from Star Power and Danger Play were there, including Nate, and the *Injury* cast and crew. Cope's family was there—even Margaret, who smiled at Dani and then looked away. Margaret's apology to Dani, given two days before, had appeared genuine, and Dani had forgiven her, but distrust and tension remained between them.

Cope led Dani to two empty seats at the head of the group of tables and motioned for her and everyone else to sit.

Nervous, she sank into the chair, wondering what he was up to now.

He looked into the crowd, back to Dani, and then again turned to the group. He took a deep breath and spoke. "Thank you for coming here to celebrate Dani's recovery with us. It's been a challenging time, and we appreciate everything you've done for us."

He faced Dani again. "When you disappeared, I was terrified I'd lost you forever. The thought of enduring each day without you turned every moment into darkness. You're the light that keeps me going. Being with you gives my life more joy and meaning than I've ever known." He reached into his pocket, pulled out a diamond ring, and kneeled before her. "Dani, will you marry me?"

Tears filled her eyes, and she could at first only nod. *Yes. Yes. Yes.* She gasped as he slipped the ring, an elegant white and yellow gold solitaire, onto her finger. After a tear-filled pause, she inhaled, settling her emotions, and shouted so everyone could hear. "Yes!"

Cheers and shouts of congratulations filled the air.

Dani inhaled and drew in the scent of the sea, the flowers and candles, and the aroma of something meaty wafting up from barbeques along the cliff face.

Astounded and touched, she contemplated the work that must have gone into putting this together. She launched herself into Cope's arms.

He caught her, hugged her, and they kissed. When he released her, Dani whispered in his ear. "I can't believe you did this. You're amazing."

"I love you, Daniella."

"I love you, too, Robert."

As the night wore on, and the stars appeared in the sky, Dani and Cope stepped away from the celebrating and walked along the beach. Feet bare, Dani picked her way through the surf, shivering in the brisk water. Cope's grip on her hand reassured her. No matter what, she could depend on him. He wouldn't leave her.

She recalled the years she'd spent seeking publicity and hoping her father would find her. Even if only in a dream, she'd seen him at last, and, if not a dream, then perhaps he'd been there all along. Maybe, he'd be with her always as he'd promised.

Now, Cope had made the same promise to her.

She hugged him. "I'm whole again, and it's because you came into my life. Daniella Grayson always needed to be in the spotlight. Daniella Copeland will want something different. After I fulfill my studio contract, I don't want to do another movie. What do you think?"

"Wherever you want to go from here, or whatever you want to do, I'll support you."

He kissed her again, and she considered the possibilities: a more active role at Star Power and more time with the children coming to the charity. Those things made her heart soar. She and Cope would have children, and she'd make sure they grew up in a loving family home. They'd have Cope's sister and brothers as aunt and uncles. Dani's heart overflowed at the prospect of giving a baby the love-filled childhood she'd never had.

Cope placed an arm around her, and she snuggled into him. They stood, facing the ocean, and watched the waves roll in to shore.

###

SAMPLE CHAPTER: *GILLIAN'S ISLAND*

Today, my life changes forever.

Gillian Foster unclipped the last clothes peg and hauled the crisp, white sheet from the line. It went into the laundry basket beside her with the rest of the bedding, all of it done for a man she'd never met.

As resort owner, she'd often done laundry for strangers when an extra pair of hands was needed, but this time, it was different. This time, it was for Daylin Quinn, the resort's new owner, and that made her every motion heavy and reluctant.

The heat didn't help put a spring in her step. The day was uncharacteristically hot, the air oppressive. It was the first of May and felt like the end of June.

She sighed and ran her fingers through her hair, which always frizzed up in humidity. She bunched it into her fist to let a passing breeze cool her neck.

The wind that had dried her sheets so quickly would also blow in a cold front. The puffy, white clouds overhead now showed hints of grey. Sooner or later, a storm would blow in. Hopefully, it wouldn't be until after Daylin had arrived safely on the island—unless it rolled in fast.

Then she could use it to her advantage and delay the visit until tomorrow. Sure, it put off the inevitable, but a storm was a legitimate reason to procrastinate.

She hefted the basket onto her hip and walked from the garden through the sunroom to the large living room. She set the basket on the floor and arched backward, rubbing her lower back.

A stereo system in the corner next to the fieldstone fireplace had a radio, and she switched it on. Eventually, there'd be a weather report.

168

Damn it, if she was forced to sell her home, why did it have to be to an arrogant developer like Daylin Quinn?

When he'd made the offer through his real estate agent, Gillian had researched him on the Internet. That had been both enlightening and infuriating.

He had a history of buying up properties, demolishing the buildings, and redeveloping the lots. It had made him a wealthy man, but the prospect of her beautiful century home being torn down nauseated her.

She envisioned a cheesy souvenir shop and tacky cabins; the porch swing gone, a snack machine in its place; the quaint restaurant preparing home-cooked meals replaced by greasy fast food. Her blood boiled as she imagined what he might do, and she wished this city boy had stayed there despite how close to her asking price he'd come.

Most of the photos she'd found of him showed a stunningly handsome man with a variety of gorgeous women on his arm—sometimes one on each arm. No mention of a wife or steady girlfriend. Not that it was any of her business, but it was a reflection of his character.

Worse still, he was an American. A New Yorker.

The locals weren't pleased when the news that the Fosters had sold the island to a foreigner spread. Most of them admitted no one living in the area had the millions required to buy the resort. Still, they considered it a betrayal that the purchaser not only wasn't from Ontario but wasn't even a Canadian.

No matter that Daylin's had been the only offer in the two years the island had been on the market. Nor did anyone care that Gillian's ex-husband had forced her to sell so he could get his half of the money. Folks simply expressed their resentment at what she'd done without regard to the extenuating circumstances.

Now he was coming to claim what was legally his.

She carried the laundry basket into the master bedroom to make the queen bed, one of the many pieces of furniture she was leaving here.

She'd already moved most of the possessions she was keeping into a storage unit on the mainland in the town of Fiddlehead. The meagre wardrobe and personal items she'd need for her month here had been transferred into a room in the staff quarters.

Daylin had contracted her to stay on for two months to show him how the resort operated. She planned to live on the island for the first month and then move to the mainland and commute to work for the second month. This would help her transition to life without her island.

The scent of the outdoors wafted from the freshly laundered sheets as she worked. The cozy comforter she spread out on the bed would provide warmth for the remaining chilly nights ahead. She arranged the decorative pillows and stepped back to survey her handiwork.

All was ready.

Daylin would probably claim this room for his own until he destroyed the place.

Stop it. You don't know that's what he wants to do. She shook her head. It wasn't being cynical if history showed that's what he'd always done.

The weather report caught her attention. She cheered and did a skip-dance when the announcer upgraded the storm watch to a warning.

She rushed to the kitchen where she'd left her cell phone and called Daylin's office.

His assistant answered and took the message. She assured Gillian she'd notify Mr. Quinn to stay in his hotel tonight and head out to the island the next morning.

Relief flooded through her as she disconnected the call, and she sent a quick thank you to whatever weather god might be responsible for this turn. Admittedly, it was silly to get so excited over a one-night reprieve. Nevertheless, the rescheduling made her heart soar.

When Daylin stepped foot on shore, the place would be his. Until then, she'd spend tonight blessedly alone, curled up in front of the fireplace with a book and a glass of wine.

First, she'd better batten down the hatches before the storm hit.

***

Daylin Quinn ended his call and started his Mercedes-Benz E-Class sedan, which sat in the hotel parking lot. He gazed up at the sky.

The sun speared through grey-tinged clouds devoid of menace. His assistant had caught him in time to abort the trip to the island, but Daylin wouldn't let a little rain spoil his plans.

Rain seemed a remote possibility anyway, judging by the sky. If he was wrong, it might hit while he was crossing the channel between mainland and island, but so what? His boat was sturdy and would get him across.

He'd waited long enough to visit his new place again. The quick walk-through before he'd bought the island was a faint memory. He had big plans to implement, and the desire to get started was an itch he had to scratch right now.

To hell with rain. Most forecasts were wrong anyway.

Light traffic on the highway ensured he'd quickly get to the marina where he'd leave his car and pick up his boat. From there, it was ten minutes to the island.

He looked forward to meeting Gillian Foster. He'd investigated the former owner of Loon Island Resort and liked what he'd seen.

She'd lovingly cared for the place even after her marriage had broken down and left her to run it alone. Her insistence on putting into the sales contract a clause to honour the reservations she'd taken before the sale had impressed him. He'd agreed to it readily.

If he ran the resort this season, he'd get a feel for the land before he made any changes. The bonus was that her pictures showed a fit, sexy body despite her hiding it under sweatshirts and baggy pants.

As he sped toward the turnoff to Loon Island Marina Road, he cranked the radio and burst into song. Anticipation and joy surged through him, and it was all he could do not to bounce on the seat like a kid on Santa's knee. The start of an important new project always gave him a thrill, and he was on his way to meet with an intriguing new woman.

Could it get any better than this?

ABOUT THE AUTHOR

Author Val Tobin lives in Newmarket, Ontario with her husband, Bob, and Scully, their cat. Website: www.valtobin.com

Other books by Val Tobin:

Paranormal Sci-Fi Thrillers
The Valiant Chronicles Series
Earthbound (prequel): A spirit becomes earthbound after refusing to cross over in order to solve her murder and prevent more deaths, some of which might be predestined.

The Experiencers (book one): A black-ops assassin atones for his brutal past by helping an alien abductee escape capture.

A Ring of Truth (book two): A rogue assassin triggers an apocalypse when he attempts to rescue a group of alien abductees.

The Valiant Chronicles books are also available as a complete set in e-book and paperback.

Romantic Suspense
Injury: A young actress at the height of her career has her personal life turned upside down when a horrifying family secret makes front-page news.

Gillian's Island: A socially anxious divorcée confronts her greatest fears when she's forced to sell her island home and falls for the dashing new owner.

About Three Authors: Poison Pen: Three wannabe authors suffering from various mental disorders find love in unexpected places when they interfere in the investigation of a colleague's murder.

Forever Young: You Again: Complications arise when an accounting tech is assigned her former lover as a client and his company's previous financial controller is found dead.

Paranormal Romance
Walk-In: A young psychic woman fights an attraction to a handsome but sceptical novelist while she battles a power-hungry sorcerer determined to make her his next conquest.

Manufactured by Amazon.ca
Bolton, ON

26598631R00104